SOUND BENDER

Lin Oliver and Theo Baker

SOUND BENDER

SCHOLASTIC PRESS ▤ NEW YORK

Copyright © 2011 by Lin Oliver and Theo Baker. All rights reserved. Published by Scholastic Press, an imprint of Scholastic Inc., *Publishers since 1920.* SCHOLASTIC, SCHOLASTIC PRESS, and associated logos are trademarks and/or registered trademarks of Scholastic Inc.

Library of Congress Cataloging-in-Publication Data

Oliver, Lin.
Sound Bender / by Lin Oliver and Theo Baker.
p. cm.
Summary: After their parents are declared dead, Leo and his brother Hollis are taken in by a wealthy but distant step-uncle, and when, on his thirteenth birthday, Leo acquires the ability to hear sounds from the past when touching certain objects, he tries to use the skill to rescue a dolphin, whatever the cost.
ISBN 978-0-545-19692-5 (alk. paper)
[1. Extrasensory perception—Fiction. 2. Brothers—Fiction. 3. Orphans—Fiction. 4. Uncles—Fiction. 5. Dolphins—Fiction. 6. Science fiction.] I. Baker, Theo.
II. Title.
PZ7.O476Sou 2011
[Fic]—dc22
2011005034

10 9 8 7 6 5 4 3 2 1   11 12 13 14 15 16/0

Printed in the U.S.A.
First printing, November 2011

The display type was set in Agency Thin.
The text type was set in Alisal.
Book design by Elizabeth B. Parisi

FOR ALAN
—L.O.

FOR SARAH
—T.B.

ACKNOWLEDGMENTS

The authors wish to thank our editors, Abigail McAden and Zachary Clark. Your insight and guidance have been invaluable. Thanks also to David Saylor and Debra Dorfman for your creative vision and leadership, and to Ellen Goldsmith-Vein and Eddie Gamarra of The Gotham Group for their unwavering support.

While *Sound Bender* is a work of fiction, the records mentioned within the book are very real and can be found with a little effort. The authors urge their readers to have a look. The characters of Kirk Lomax and Jay Lylo were inspired by the lives of two real and most fascinating people: Alan (and his father, John) Lomax and John Lilly. The authors hope their readers will investigate them further.

Finally, the authors are grateful for our family and friends, as well as every independent record store in the world, and all of the serious collectors who strive every day to uncover the music buried all around us.

CHAPTER 1

The blast of the car horn shattered the predawn silence. From my bedroom window, I watched the black limousine pull up to the curb and come to a stop in front of my building. The clock on my bedside table said 5:50 a.m. The stupid car was early. Steam was rising thickly from its hood and the icy gutter water glowed red from the brake lights.

I closed my eyes tight, hoping the limo would disappear, vanish into the morning fog. It was here to take me away . . . not just from my apartment, but from my entire life as I knew it . . . like an evil monster sent to gobble me up.

Another blast from the car horn pierced the silence, startling me, and my eyes flew open just in time to see a burly man with a black mustache get out of the limo and disappear into the lobby of our building.

He was coming for us.

This was real.

For two weeks, I had imagined this moment — or mostly, how to avoid it. When they came for us, I would resist. Run. Scurry down the fire escape. Assume a new identity as a Bolivian cowboy or sneak into a Shaolin temple and become a kung fu monk. Anything to avoid getting into that car. But now that the moment was upon me, I didn't run. All I did was whisper to my sleeping brother, Hollis, "They're here."

"What do I care?" he muttered, pulling the pillow over his head. "I'm not going."

"Hollis, try not to be such a jerk for once."

He didn't answer. Didn't move a muscle. He just lay there like a mummy wrapped in his sheet.

"We don't have a choice," I snapped at him, tugging at the corner of his blanket. "Move it. We can't stay here alone."

"Guess what, Leo. I can. And I'm staying."

Truthfully, I did see his point. This was our room in our apartment on 91st Street on the Upper West Side of New York. It was the only room we'd ever known. In the only apartment we'd ever lived in. And that car was coming to take us away forever.

It was unfair. No one ever asked us if we wanted to leave. No one ever asks a kid anything. Actually, our parents did, but they were gone now. And I wasn't a kid anymore — I was almost thirteen.

Four heavy knocks on our door, then a man's booming voice.

"Leo Lomax! Hollis Lomax! Time to hit the road!" The driver's voice was thunderous, the kind of voice you don't mess with.

"Shhh," Hollis whispered, suddenly sitting up in bed and clutching Trunkie, his stuffed elephant. He hadn't slept with Trunkie in years. "Pretend we're not here."

It was too late for that. A key was turning in the lock and instinctively, like a wolf guarding its den, I raced to the front door. As I got there, I saw a large, hairy arm push open the door. It wasn't just your normal large, hairy arm, either. It was missing a big chunk of flesh just above the wrist, leaving a yellowish scarred cavity where the living tissue should have been. A split second later, the limo driver poked his face in, a chewed-up red plastic straw hanging out the side of his mouth.

"You can't come in here," I said, trying to sound like my father.

"Lighten up, kid. Your uncle Crane gave me the key. Get your stuff."

"My brother's still asleep." I was trying to stall, but he didn't buy it.

"I'll wake him," he said. "No problem."

I looked again at his forearm, my eyes homing in on the missing chunk. It was impossible not to stare at the hairless, pus-colored hole.

"I'll get him," I said. "He's a delicate sleeper."

"Suit yourself, kid. The boss says I got to treat you like princes. What happened . . . somebody die and make you punks royalty?"

"Actually someone did die. Our parents."

The minute the words were out of my mouth, I regretted saying them. But our parents' death was all so new, the grief so overwhelming, that I hadn't learned how to hold it in yet.

"Tough break," the driver said. "Tough for the boss, too. He don't like kids much."

The boss was our uncle Crane Rathbone, my dad's stepbrother who we barely knew. According to our parents' will, he was going to take care of us from now on.

As I went to our room to get Hollis, I passed my parents' bedroom where I still half expected to see my dad sitting in his beat-up leather chair reading the *New York Times*. Instead, all I saw were piles of their unopened mail, a sad reminder that they weren't coming back. So weird how your life can totally change in fourteen days.

Hollis, being his usual stubborn self, refused to get out of bed, refused to get dressed, refused to do anything. I grabbed his Mets sweatshirt from the floor, yanked it over his head, and threw some clothes into his duffel. Then I dragged him to his feet and pushed him by the neck while carrying both our bags into the hall.

The driver reached out and snatched our luggage with one hand like he was picking up a bag of nothing. That arm might be missing a chunk, but it was still powerful. I followed him down the flight of stairs out to the street, a reluctant Hollis tagging along behind. It was cold outside.

The driver opened the limo door and pointed to the backseat.

"Welcome to your new life, boys," he said, spitting the red gnarled-up straw into the gutter. "Get in."

I watched the straw rush downstream and get lodged behind a battered Elmo doll that was lying facedown in the icy water. Some poor kid was probably crying his eyes out, wondering where he had dropped his Elmo. Growing up is a bummer, I thought. I wished I could tell that kid it gets easier, but it doesn't.

I didn't want a new life. I liked my old life fine. I liked my block. I liked Yaffa's little store where I bought my black licorice. I liked Luigi's Pizza, where my best friend, Trevor, and I always stopped after school to get a pepperoni slice. I even liked the crazy man who was always walking up and down our street yelling, "Hallelujah."

"Hey, check this out, Leo." Hollis had suddenly come alive and was peering inside the limo. "Iced Cokes for breakfast."

I stuck my head inside the car. It was lit with purple neon that made the leather seats glow like those iridescent blind fish that live at the bottom of the ocean. A silver cup filled with red and white mints sat on the wooden seat divider, and in the cup holders were two icy glass bottles of Coke. It was pretty deluxe in there, and if there's anyone who loves deluxe, it's my brother, Hollis. The kid is only eleven, and he already subscribes to *Yachting* magazine.

Hollis dove into the backseat of the car, put his feet up on a velvet ledge, and opened one of the Cokes. I threw my backpack onto the carpet and followed him in. The driver slammed the door shut behind me and just like that, we left our neighborhood forever.

5

I had only met our uncle Crane five or six times in my whole life, and I knew very little about him. Only that he traveled all over the world and was rich enough to afford black limos and weird drivers and chilled Cokes whenever you wanted one. I hadn't seen him since I was in the fourth grade, when he came for dinner, and that was over three years ago. All I remembered about that night was that he kept clicking his diamond pinkie ring against the wooden arm of his chair. *Click, click, click* throughout the whole meal. By the time dessert came, I couldn't wait to get away from that sound.

Our car sped along the FDR Drive toward Canal Street and then the Brooklyn Bridge. Hollis was busy pushing buttons, opening and closing every window, flicking lights on and off, and raising and lowering the seats. I felt my behind growing warm and I shifted uncomfortably in my seat. Hollis noticed.

"I put the auto butt warmer on." He grinned.

"Well, turn it off, chief," I said. "My butt warms itself."

Hollis laughed. It was the first time I'd heard him laugh in what felt like years.

I noticed the driver checking us out in the rearview mirror.

"What's your name?" I asked him, feeling like I had to say something.

"Stump," he answered.

And that was it for our conversation. Stump was obviously a man of few words.

As we got onto the Brooklyn Bridge to leave Manhattan, I leaned my head back against the leather seat and listened to the rhythmic *bump, ba bump, ba bump* of the tires running along the concrete bridge dividers, like a drumbeat in my head. Reaching into my backpack, I pulled out the headphones and mini recorder Dad had given me for my twelfth birthday. I turned on the recorder and listened. Every sound came alive and echoed loudly in my ears . . . the sniffling of the driver, the mechanical gears of the seats shifting back and forth, even my own breathing, all flowing with the rhythm. *Bump, ba bump, ba bump.*

"Hey, you recording?" Stump asked, frowning at me in the rearview mirror. "I don't like people recording me without my permission."

"He's just a sound nut," Hollis blurted. "My weirdo brother records everything, even the garbage truck backing up."

"Shut up," I whispered to Hollis. "I do what I do. He doesn't need to know."

"You're just like Dad, Leo. Always recording with that stupid thing. What's the point?"

"I like it, that's the point."

"Fine, and I like this."

He pushed a button and opened the sunroof, letting in a blast of freezing air and a million screaming sounds that nearly blew my ears off and definitely ruined my recording. He knew that it would. He was just being a pain, as usual.

"Hollis, I'm going to tell M —"

I almost said *Mom*, until I realized that she wasn't there to turn to.

Hollis rode the rest of the way with his head poking out of the sunroof while I sat back and listened to the sounds of the neighborhoods changing.

We got off the expressway somewhere in Brooklyn and wound through small streets lined with fruit stalls, butcher shops, and signs in Polish. We turned off the avenue and soon we were bumping over potholes in a run-down area. I looked out at the vacant lots and crumbling boarded-up buildings. The car stopped at an intersection, and out of nowhere, a junkyard dog clawed a chain-link fence five feet from my window, lunging at our car like he wanted to eat our faces off.

Hollis dove back into the car and closed the sunroof as fast as he could.

"That's one nasty dog," Hollis said.

"He's got to be," I answered. "This is a nasty neighborhood."

"Hey, Leo," Hollis said, sounding suddenly younger than his sixth-grade self. "This couldn't be it, could it? Where we're going to live?"

"Don't be so dense. Uncle Crane's rich. Why would he live here?"

The car turned a corner onto an even shabbier block. I cracked the window open to get a better look. The air smelled rancid, like a pot of old hot dog water that had been sitting on the stove for a week.

"Close up that window, kid," Stump ordered. "Can't have the car reeking of week-old salami. I drive a lot of VIP clients in here."

We were in front of a dilapidated one-story factory building. On its roof was a giant sign with a picture of a half-eaten salami that said FINKELSTEIN FAMILY SALAMI FACTORY, ESTABLISHED 1931.

I was so busy staring at the place, thinking about all the disgusting things that must be going on in there, that I didn't notice our car had made a U-turn and pulled up in front of a filthy brick building that took up the rest of the block. It stretched seven stories into the sky with hundreds of windows that were so grimy they looked totally black. The only color at all came from a flock of ratty white seagulls perched in the crevices of the brick.

Stump turned off the ignition and popped open the trunk.

Hollis glared at me. "Leo, you said . . ."

The rest of his sentence was drowned out by my own thoughts. Please, don't let this be the place. Please make this all go away. Please, Mom and Dad, come get us. Now! Hurry! Please . . .

My mind was screaming but my face was still. The only movement I allowed myself was a sideways glance at the building. Painted in inconspicuous silver letters were the words *Crane's Mysteries*.

Crane. Uncle Crane. Oh no.

Stump got out and held open the door. "Out with you, kiddo. And get the little guy. The boss don't like to wait."

I took a deep breath. The smell of salami was everywhere. I held my hand out for Hollis and pulled him from the back of the limo.

"Come on, chief," I said to him, trying to sound reassuring. "We can do this."

Hollis could be a pain in the butt, but he was my brother. All we had was each other, and this new place, this building in the middle of nowhere that smelled of salami and seagulls.

This was it.

This was home.

CHAPTER 2

A short, muscular man with an incredibly precise crew cut came running out of the building to greet us. His hair was buzzed so flat on top that it looked like a power lawn mower had run over it.

"Hullo, boys. Come in, come in!" he yelled in a thick accent.

"They're all yours, Klevko," Stump said, tossing our duffel bags onto the ground. He got back into the limo, rolled up the tinted driver's side window, and sped off. Apparently, he wasn't much on good-byes.

"Don't mind Stump," the man named Klevko said. "He is good driver but not friendly, like me. I am Klevko, your friend. Now hurry, boys. My boss, your uncle Crane, he waits." Klevko hoisted our duffel bags onto his strong back. Even though it was the dead of winter, his tight elastic shirt was drenched in sweat.

"You have beautiful rooms," he said, putting one of his sweaty hands on me and one on Hollis, guiding us toward the building. "My wife, Olga, cleaned them for you. No more spiders."

Hollis shuddered at the very mention of spiders. He is definitely not a big fan of the bug world, never has been. Me, I kind of like bugs, especially cockroaches because they make this little *tick, tick, tick* sound with their wings when they scurry around in the dark, which I've actually recorded. It sounds cool, like when you click one of your fingernails against your thumbnail.

Klevko seemed nice enough, although I could have done without the blond hairs sticking out of his nostrils. Ditto for the sweaty chest hair poking out of his collar.

"You are Leo," he said, pointing a finger at me. "You look like your father, Kirk. You are short and have fat cheeks like him."

He grabbed one of my cheeks hard and squeezed it, then tousled Hollis's hair with his other large, sweaty hand.

"And you are Hollis, yes? You have pretty green eyes like your mother, what was her name?"

"Yolanda," Hollis snapped, pushing Klevko's hand off his head.

"Yes, Yolanda. She was beautiful woman. You are tough like she was. I like you."

Klevko slapped his hand against his belly and gave out a loud laugh that sounded like he was gargling and clearing his throat at the same time. We followed him into the building lobby, if you could even call it a lobby. It was more like a cave, moist and gray, with a rusty caged elevator at one end.

"This is my elevator," Klevko said. "It is dangerous. Only my boy, Dmitri, can ride alone. You must always go with me. If not, maybe you lose a finger."

We got in and Klevko pulled the ancient brass grate across the opening. It slammed shut with a rattle that echoed throughout the elevator shaft. I noticed a small door on the side of the elevator, maybe three feet high, which was cracked open. A strong smell wafted out of it. Was it cabbage? Peeking inside, I could barely make out the front room of a small basement apartment with peeling wallpaper and framed pictures of men with mustaches. I heard the sounds of a fork clanking against a plate and what sounded like a pig eating his slop. I poked my head farther in. I saw a boy about a year or two younger than me, maybe about Hollis's age, wearing a dark red shirt and sitting at a table, stuffing his face with a plate of brown and yellow foods. So that was the smell . . . not cabbage but sausage and sauerkraut.

The boy sensed me staring at him, because he looked up and stared back at me. He wiped his greasy face with his forearm and snorted out of his nose.

"That is Dmitri, my boy," Klevko said. "He knows how to work all the machines. He is important to Crane's business. He is your friend. Especially for you," he said, pointing to Hollis.

I sidled over to Hollis and pinched his arm.

"Meet your new best buddy," I whispered.

Hollis punched me in the arm, hard, in exactly the same spot where I'd pinched him. Klevko saw us and laughed.

"You boys like to play games, too? Dmitri likes to play games. He likes to play where you put a bag, you know, eh, eh, a sack on your head, and then dodge punches from other friends. It is Dmitri's favorite."

He let out another one of those combo throat-clearing gargle–laughs. Klevko closed the little door.

Hollis shot me his *what-is-going-on-here* look, and I just shrugged. Our new life was coming at us hard, and we were going to have to learn some new games.

"Okay," Klevko said. "We go up now. Crane waits."

He pulled a lever and the elevator lurched up with a jerk so strong it sent Hollis and me slamming into the walls. About thirty seconds later, the elevator stopped just as suddenly.

"We are here. The penthouse," Klevko said, and slid the gate across.

An immense room, blindingly bright, opened before us. It was sleek and modern, decorated with black-and-white zebra-striped furniture, expensive-looking glass tables, and dozens of large marble sculptures. The ceiling was so high that a ten-foot statue of a bearded man raising an eagle over his head actually looked small in the room.

The size of the room made me feel dizzy, like I had water in my ears, but Hollis stepped right out of the elevator and strutted around the room like he belonged there. He marched over to the floor-to-ceiling windows and looked out at the view of the Brooklyn waterfront and a wooden boardwalk that ran along the East River. Not a nice waterfront with coffee shops and sailboats and stuff, but the kind where ratty seagulls sit on ratty wooden posts and flap their ratty wings.

Hollis flopped himself down in one of the zebra-striped chairs next to the huge marble statue, reached out, and took a handful of fancy cashews from a dish on the glass table.

"You're as stiff as one of these statues, bro," Hollis said. "Come in and make yourself at home."

"Quiet. I hear something."

It was a faint voice talking in the next room. A deep, lizardy voice, speaking in a foreign language — the kind of voice that demanded to be listened to.

"What is it?" Hollis asked.

"It's Uncle Crane. You hear him?"

"No." Hollis barely looked up, just grabbed another handful of nuts and tossed them in.

I tried to locate the voice, but the place was so large that every sound echoed off the walls and shot back at me. Crane's voice was everywhere. Then I saw him, at the far side of the room behind a statue of a Greek athlete throwing what looked like a Frisbee. All I could see was the back of his bald head, a cell phone pressed up against his ear. He was just as I remembered, immaculately dressed in rich-looking clothes, today a gray turtleneck peeking out of a maroon sport coat. In his phone hand, I saw that pinkie ring, flooded with diamonds.

"There he is," I said to Hollis. "Think we should go say hi?"

"You can," Hollis snapped. "I'm eating."

He made me so mad when he acted this way. It was like he'd decided that we were both on our own, and that he was going to do better without me.

"You're such a brat," I said to him. I felt myself tearing up and I hated myself for that, and hated Hollis for making me feel this way. "I have to do everything for you, because you just sit there and — "

I heard the cell phone snap closed. I looked over toward Crane, but he was no longer behind the statue. Footsteps clicked on the wood floors, echoing off the walls, coming toward us. Getting louder.

"Knock off the attitude, Leo," Hollis said, standing up. "Try to make a decent impression for once."

The footsteps stopped before they reached us.

"Klevko!" the lizardy voice hissed.

Klevko bolted out from behind us and shot across the room. I saw Crane take him by the elbow and move him behind another statue, this one of a naked woman holding a lion cub. I couldn't see them talking, but I could catch little bits of their conversation: "You fool . . . disappointed . . . says it's not a real bone . . . three hundred thousand . . . out of your pay . . . they're here? . . . you didn't tell me . . . we'll talk about this later . . . donkey . . . buffoon . . . "

Suddenly, Crane burst out from behind the statue and strode directly toward us, his arms outstretched. He looked nothing like our father. Our dad was short and wore rumpled clothes and carried a beat-up old leather briefcase to and from Columbia University where he taught world music. His students loved him because he could tell you anything you wanted to know about African thumb pianos or Mongolian throat singers or Micronesian nose flutes. From the looks of his fancy clothes, I was pretty sure Uncle Crane had zero interest in nose flutes.

"My boys, my boys!" he said, walking over to us, the leather in his expensive shoes squeaking. "Klevko is a buffoon. A terrible employee, but I love him dearly. He should have told me you were here."

He took Hollis and me in his arms and placed a hand on each of our shoulders. I got the hand with the diamond pinkie ring. He pulled me to him and his leathery cologne burned my nostrils.

"My boys, it breaks my heart that it took this . . . this terrib—oh, it's too horrible—this wretched accident to bring us together. I have not been in your lives, but I have loved you dearly from afar."

He paused a moment, as if he were expecting both of us to say, "That's okay, Uncle Crane, we love you ever so much." I couldn't bring myself to say anything of the kind, so I just muttered, "Thank you for taking us, Uncle Crane."

"Do you even remember me, Leo? Your father has entrusted you to me, and I am going to take care of you. My business has made me a wealthy man, and I am going to see that you get the best of everything."

Crane got to one knee, and Hollis shot me a look over the top of his shiny head, a look that said, this may not be so bad after all. Like I said, that Hollis likes his luxuries.

"This will not be easy, Leo, but we will—oh, look at your stubby fingers, just like your father's. My poor brother, my poor brother. But you boys must be starving and exhausted—Klevko!" Crane thankfully let go of my hand—which is not *that* stubby—and stood up.

"Yes, sir?"

"Get Olga, call her. Tell her to make that dish. You know, the brown and yellow one, something a child will like."

Klevko nodded and disappeared into the elevator. Crane turned to us, and gave me a pinch on the cheek. "So, first order of business. We've got to keep Leo's fat cheeks from spreading to the rest of his body, eh?"

Hollis, the traitor, chuckled. "Leo doesn't like it when you call him chubby."

"Neither did his father." Crane laughed. "He would get so angry, his chubby little face would turn absolutely crimson."

"I'm pretty athletic," I said. "It's mostly muscle."

"That was very insensitive of me, Leo," Crane said, looking at me kindly. "I understand what it must feel like to be a husky boy like you."

"So your apartment is really great," I said, eager to change the subject.

"Yeah, it's totally cool," Hollis agreed, almost too enthusiastically.

"*Cool?*" Crane repeated. "I don't approve of that word. Cool is a setting on air-conditioning. Not a word for the priceless art and artifacts you see around you."

"Artifacts?" Hollis asked.

"Precious handmade objects from an earlier time."

"Yeah, Hollis, like the Schwinn Black Phantom bike from the '50s," I said. "My best friend Trevor's dad has one and it's so sweet."

Uncle Crane threw back his head and laughed.

"Leo, a bicycle is hardly in the same class with what I collect and sell. This entire building is filled with rare items that are worth millions."

"*Millions?*" Hollis said, lighting up at the sound of his favorite word. "Wow."

Crane nodded.

"And since we're on the topic, boys, I do have one rule. My things are my things. And your things are your things. If you are thinking of touching my things, do not. And I won't touch yours. I find that reasonable. Now, would you like to see your rooms?"

Crane didn't wait for an answer. He set off across the giant room, walking so fast that Hollis and I had to jog every now and then to keep up with him. We crossed what I swear was a bridge made of glass that led to another huge room, this one with a floor-to-ceiling flat-screen television on one wall and on the other, hundreds of different swords — samurai swords, scimitar swords, medieval swords.

"Keep up, Leo," Crane said. "I don't like laggers."

We crossed another glass bridge and entered into a third room filled with Native American totem poles, a wall of African masks, and a forty-foot dugout canoe that hung from invisible wires on the ceiling. Up ahead, Uncle Crane and Hollis were heading toward a long hallway. I sprinted up to them.

"Hey, Uncle Crane," I hollered. "What was all that stuff?"

Crane raised an eyebrow.

"*Stuff?* Stuff, my precious Leo, is what is inside of stuffed animals. Those objects are the reason you will now have such a luxurious life. I buy and sell rare antiques and artifacts from around the world. Every item is without estimate. And now, gentlemen, without further ado . . . "

Crane pointed to two doors at the end of the hallway.

"The room on the right is for Hollis, the one on the left is for you, Leo. I flipped a coin to assign them — I am told that boys your age like to fight about everything. There'll be no need for that here."

Hollis and I both took off down the hall. Hollis is fast so he was already inside his room by the time I reached mine. Uncle Crane stayed by my side as I opened the door.

Whoa. I had never seen anything like it.

All the furniture, even the bed, was suspended from the walls   it it looked like everything was floating. There
         g on any surface, not a piece of paper or a book
       it. Or a window. It was the total opposite of my old
      with Hollis, which was filled with my tape recorders,
    s's instruments, our old art projects all over the walls,

booby traps made of wire and string, toy cars on the floor that you could slip on and break your neck, and a pile of clothes known as "Mount Everest Part II."

"My room's from the future," I said, running my hand over the shiny metal drawers that protruded from the white walls.

Crane nodded proudly. "Prefabricated modular units from Denmark. Absolute functionality. I ordered them especially for you boys."

"My room is definitely cool," Hollis said. Then, noticing Crane's disapproving look, he added, "I mean is definitely as *nice*."

"Hey, Uncle Crane. Where's my stuff?" I asked. Again, the disapproving look from Crane. "Oh, I mean my *belongings*."

"Relax, little Leo, my staff is bringing everything over. Klevko has already brought your bags from the car. I'll leave you both to unpack. If you need anything, use the buzzer. Press number thirty-four to summon Klevko, and number thirty-five to summon Dmitri."

"How do we summon you?" I asked.

"You don't. After you've settled in, I'll have Klevko buzz you for lunch. You'll enjoy Olga's cooking. I asked her to make a cake for your birthday, Leo."

"But my birthday isn't till tomorrow."

Crane raised an eyebrow.

"Then my information is incorrect. The attorneys for your parents' estate told me that your birthday is January nineteenth."

"Um, it is, yeah."

"Leo, today is January nineteenth."

What? I couldn't believe it. I must have lost track of the days. It wasn't surprising with everything that I'd been through lately, but I couldn't believe I forgot my own birthday.

"Happy birthday, bro," Hollis said. "I guess."

"Which reminds me," Crane said, "a messenger brought a package for you today. A filthy fellow, smelled like a goat. He said it was to be delivered on your birthday."

"What kind of package?" I asked, wondering who even knew I was here.

"I have no idea," Crane answered. "I asked Klevko to leave it on your bed."

I glanced over at my bed and there it was, a tattered yellow envelope tied with an unraveling piece of twine. The package looked like it had been trampled by a herd of buffalo.

"I bet it's from Trevor," Hollis said. Trevor Davis had been my best friend since kindergarten and he would never forget my birthday, but this was definitely not his work. Being a scientist, he's got very methodical habits, much too precise to put together a sloppy package like that.

A cell phone rang in one of Crane's pockets.

"Nee how," he answered, and then turning to us said, "I'll have Dmitri summon you in exactly one half hour." With that, he spun around and headed down the hall, conversing just as easily in Chinese as he did in English.

Hollis disappeared into his room to check out the electronics. His door shut. We had shared a room all of our lives. My old life was gone.

Alone in my room now, I picked up the package from my bed and studied it. Its age-worn paper was smooth in my hand. It was addressed to me, but the handwriting was definitely not Trevor's. I knew that handwriting. Knew it as well I know my own. That green ink from the fountain pen, the fancy curly *L* of my name.

Only one person wrote like that. It was my father's handwriting. No mistaking it.

Without realizing it, I hugged the package to my chest. Whatever it contained was the last gift from my father to me. A chill crept over me as I ran my fingers over the words. They simply said: *TO LEO LOMAX. TO BE OPENED ON HIS 13TH BIRTHDAY. WITHOUT FAIL.*

CHAPTER 3

My dad was always great at giving birthday presents. When I was three, he gave me a red plastic turntable with records that only had sound effects on them — wolves howling, thunder rumbling, doors opening and creaking shut. For my eighth birthday he gave me this weird contraption called a vocoder, which, when I talked into it, made my voice sound like a robot. Trevor and I had a great time with that thing. But the best was when I was ten — he gave me a stealth voice recorder watch, which Mrs. Rose, my fourth grade teacher, took away from me because I recorded David Platt's stomach making digestive sounds after eating the school tacos. My dad actually went to school and told Mrs. Rose that a child's curiosity should never be punished, then pulled me out of 97th Street School and put me in the Academy of Sciences and Arts, where I still go.

As I sat on my new bed in my new spaceship of a room, I wondered what kind of birthday present could be in the yellow envelope. How did he know he wouldn't be here to give it to me himself? Did he sense that he and my mom would die in a plane crash three weeks before my thirteenth birthday? To me, it still felt like they were just on a trip, and any minute they would walk into the room and take us home.

My mom and dad often traveled to remote islands and small villages so my dad could record the music of the native tribes. Every now and then he took me. On one trip, the one where I saw a bear get sacrificed, the plane engine caught fire and we had to make an emergency landing on a dirt road. For the past two weeks, I had been replaying that moment over and over in my mind, wondering if that's what happened to them, only this time they didn't make it.

No one, not even Hollis or me, knew for certain the exact circumstances of their death. They had gone to Antarctica. My mom is — I mean was — a famous violinist. She and her string quartet had been asked to play a concert for the lonely scientists down in Antarctica. After the concert, my parents decided to take a small plane to look at the glaciers and icebergs. But the plane never returned to the base. That was three weeks ago. Two weeks ago, they stopped searching for them, and declared them dead. I never got a chance to search for them, or to even say good-bye.

Looking down at the battered yellow envelope, I realized I had been holding it in my lap for fifteen minutes, lost in thought about my parents, doing what I had been doing constantly since I heard the news — trying to reverse time, to turn back the clock, so I could bring them home.

I wanted to open the package and yet I didn't want to open it. My heart was pounding in my ears as I untied the knotted twine. Suddenly, I heard footsteps in the hall. I was half expecting Hollis to walk in, so I quickly shoved the envelope under my pillow. I didn't want him to know that the package was from Dad. Not yet. Right now, this was only for me.

Outside the room, the footsteps broke into a run. I rushed to the doorway and poked my head into the shadowy hall.

"Hollis?"

There was no answer.

"Anyone there?"

I went back to my bed, took the envelope from beneath the pillow, and carefully opened it. I'm not sure what I was expecting, but inside, I found a letter from my dad. The paper was smudged all over with splotches of green ink. It was dated January 19, the year of my first birthday.

Dear Leo,

When you were born one year ago, it was the happiest day of my life. Now you are thirteen and close to becoming a man. I hope I have taught you to always listen to that little voice inside of you. The voice that tells you to ask questions, to work hard, to become yourself. That little voice, Leo, is you.

This letter is not to offer you advice about your future, but to tell you about your past, about your birth and the first

days after. I am putting it all down in writing now because
memory fades and changes with time — and I want you to
have a perfect record of what happened on the island the day
you were born.

I put the letter down and rubbed my eyes. I didn't understand what he was talking about. I already knew everything
there was to know about my birth. I was born on the island
of Manhattan, January 19th, at 7:42 p.m., weighing six
pounds seven ounces. It was all written down on the birth
announcement my parents sent out with a picture of me in
a ridiculous bunny hat with fluffy bunny ears. So what else
was there to know?

I read on.

As a graduate student, I had become fascinated with
the existence of unexplored islands in the South Pacific,
off Papua New Guinea. Some scholars believed that there
were tribes on those islands who had never been contacted by
the outside world, tribes who had been alone for ten thou-
sand years or more. Ten thousand years! Wherever there are
people, Leo, there is music. And those people who had been
alone for all that time, with no outside influences — can
you imagine what their music would sound like? I had to
meet them.

Your mother agreed to accompany me on a six-month
excursion to find them. It wasn't until we arrived in the
South Pacific that we discovered she was pregnant with
you. She felt fine, and wanted to continue our travels, so we

decided to stay and return home several months before your birth.

We hired a boat and set sail. On the thirty-third day, I spotted a small tropical island, only a few miles across. We anchored our boat, and through my binoculars, I saw a man standing on the sandy shore, painted yellow from head to toe and wearing a headdress made of feathers and plants. He was looking at the boat. Watching us watch him.

As we rowed to shore, a large crowd of islanders gathered. Slowly they came toward us. They touched our skin, smelled our hair, looked in our pockets, but when we tried to communicate with them, they didn't understand at all.

In an attempt to show them who we were, your mother took out her violin and played a short sonata by Bach. The moment she started playing, everyone froze. They huddled close to her and swayed back and forth to the music. I looked at the man in yellow, who was the shaman, or holy man, and our eyes locked. I believe that for the first time, we recognized each other as humans.

My throat got tight with emotion as I read the letter. I could almost hear my father's voice as I read. I imagined him sitting on my bed and telling me a strange and wonderful story, just like he used to do when I couldn't sleep. Every word sounded just like him. But I still didn't see what these island people had to do with me.

I stretched out on the bed and tried to get comfortable, but it was hard as a rock. Like everything else in Uncle

Crane's apartment, the bed looked great but didn't make you feel exactly welcome. I crumpled the pillow under my head as best I could, and went on reading.

When your mom finished playing, the islanders went into their huts and returned carrying bamboo flutes, gourds, sticks, strange string instruments, and snakeskin drums. A woman with a small flute put it to her lips — and this I'd never believe unless I'd seen it with my own eyes — she played note for note the Bach sonata. A young boy rubbed hollow sticks together to make a rhythm, and everybody with an instrument joined in. The holy man sang the melody in a high, beautiful voice. He sounded like a bird. Then everyone else began to sing — kids, elders, parents, teenagers. Even your mother. I'll never forget that moment.

Music is truly the bridge between people, Leo, and that experience immediately connected us with the islanders. As the days passed, we began to understand their words and language, which worked more like music than anything else. We stopped going back to the boat at night and stayed with them, sleeping under the stars on beds of reeds. We saw no wars, no fights, no stealing, and no lying.

At night, they gathered around the fire to sing songs about the "old ones," the ancestor spirits who offered advice and courage.

Days turned into months, and your mother's stomach grew until we could see the outline of your feet when you rolled over in her belly. It was time to return to New York so you could

*be born. As we were leaving, the tribe's medicine woman put
her hands on your mom's stomach, then spoke in an alarmed
voice. She communicated to us that she felt . . . no . . . she
knew it was dangerous for your mother to travel — you were
ready to come out. The medicine woman fed your mom special herbs and roots and made her a nest inside her hut. Your
mother rested there for a week, and at last, you were born,
one month early but a perfect, beautiful boy.*

I couldn't believe what I was reading! There had to be a
mistake. They told me I had been born in New York, up the
street from our apartment, in the same hospital where
Hollis was born. Why hadn't they told me about the island?
How could they have kept this a secret all these years? I was
starting to get a very creepy feeling about this, as if I had
been born with some sort of curse, as if I wasn't who I
thought I was. I remembered how Bruce Lee had a curse
that ran in his family that his dad passed on to him.

Could I, Leo Lomax, be the victim of some ancient tribal
curse? No wonder my heart was racing. My hands shook as
I read the rest of the letter.

*The night of your birth there was a festival with food and
fire and singing and dancing. It was a naming ceremony for
you. The shaman placed you inside a hollow drum, and
throughout the night, a dozen young men and women sang
the entire history of the island to you. The shaman went into
a trance and danced feverishly for hours, then collapsed in
the sand. He slept all day and night, motionless. A few*

younger men sat by him and fanned him with reeds and wiped his forehead with wet leaves.

The next morning, the shaman startled awake and told us that your ancestral name had come to him in a dream. He took you in his arms and walked toward the sea. As the first rays of the sun streaked into the gray sky, he began to chant and, in the most beautiful song I have ever heard, sang your ancestral name, over and over and over until the sun was directly overhead.

I did not understand what your name meant. From the drawing the shaman made in the sand, it seemed to mean something like "bridge to other worlds." But since our return, I have studied my recordings, and I believe that the literal translation means "bent sound," or "sound bender." The holy man warned us not to reveal your ancestral name to you until you were ready to hear it, until you were thirteen years old, the age when tribal boys are welcomed into manhood.

When you were strong enough, we left the island and came back to New York. The rest you know. We told no one where you were born, because we swore to protect the privacy of the tribe and their untouched, beautiful way of life. I am telling you this now because it is time for you to hear your ancestral name, time to take yourself seriously and learn to hear that small voice inside your head. Remember, you were born on an island half a world away, and though you live in New York, a part of you still lives on that island with your "other family." You are Leo Lomax, but you are also Sound Bender.

In the year that I have known you, my son, you have brought me great joy. May it always be so.

Dad

P.S. I have included a recording of your ancestral name on the blue disc in this envelope. It is the only recording of it. I'll come find you today to help you listen to it. In the event that I am not able to, you must find a way to hear it. But always keep the disc a secret. Tell no one about your history. It is for you and you alone.

When I put down the letter, my head was swimming, all the images of that island swirling in my mind. I took a few deep breaths, then the feelings hit with the force of a hurricane. I felt angry and confused and afraid and lonely. All my emotions were crashing like waves inside me and I wanted someone to take them out on, someone to yell at, someone to blame.

Without thinking, I punched the pillow, then picked up the yellow envelope and threw it hard across my room. It hit the sleek dresser drawers and as it fell to the floor, something slid out. Something shiny. It was the blue disc. It was the size of one of my dad's old records, the ones he called 45s with the big holes in the middle. But it wasn't like any record I had ever seen before. The hole was much smaller, and the entire disc was shiny and metallic blue, with no writing on it anywhere.

I reached down and picked it up, aware that it was the

last gift my dad would ever give me. It was floppy and delicate and warbled in my hand. As I stood there, I began to feel a little light-headed. Could it be that the disc was almost glowing, or was it just my imagination? I stared at the blue surface, but really it wasn't blue, it was flickering with these ripples of white light, probably a reflection of the overhead light from the ceiling. I was growing dizzier, so I just kept gazing at the disc to steady myself. The ripples of white light were growing brighter and brighter, and turning into whirlpools, becoming bigger and bigger until the entire disc was a shimmering circle of light, too bright, too painful to look at. I realized that I was hearing every single noise around me all at once — the humming of the light fixture, a dog barking far in the distance, the *thunk ka thunk* of tires passing over potholes in the street. I looked at the white walls around me, but they were almost transparent, covered with those ripples and whirlpools of electricity. Spinning around and around. Then a new sound began to rise in my head. A kind of pulsing feeling, like when you have water in your ears. It grew louder and louder until it was all I could hear. The room was blinding. Time seemed to stop. I felt beyond anyone's help. Everything was shining and spinning and pulsing.

I don't know what happened next, but all I could sense were the sounds of long, slow waves crashing. It was so peaceful, just listening to those slow waves crash and get sucked back out to sea.

I had a strange feeling that I was traveling.

CHAPTER 4

When I opened my eyes, I was on the floor of my room, facedown, head throbbing. Someone had his hand on my shoulder and was shaking it. From the corner of my eye, I saw that it was that boy from the basement apartment. I popped up and spun around, and I must have startled him, because he jumped back and struck something of a kung fu pose.

"Easy there, tiger. I'm on your side," I said to him, rubbing my face, trying to remember exactly what had happened to me. "You're Dmitri, right?"

"Yes, I'm Dmitri." Slowly, he lowered his hands from the attack position. "My father tells me you are Leo."

He walked over and sat down on my bed, right on the pillow. Even in my confused state, I was still alert enough to know that it is gross for someone you barely know to put his butt where you sleep.

"Dmitri, can you do me a big favor, man, and get off my bed? You're right on the pillow."

He looked a little offended, and as he got up slowly and groaned, I realized he sounded and looked like a half-size version of his father, Klevko. He was about Hollis's age, but where Hollis is thin, this guy had little bulging muscles like a mini-man. He wore a white tank top and was already growing hair under his arms. Judging from his father's chest and nose hair problem, I suspected Dmitri had inherited the hairy gene. His eyes darted around my room, like he was looking for something.

"Dmitri, um, what are you doing in my room?"

"Crane sent me. It's time for lunch."

"You ever hear of knocking?"

"I did knock. You didn't answer, so I came in."

"I didn't answer because I was asleep."

"Why do you sleep on the floor like a dog?"

That was a good question. Why was I asleep on the floor? I didn't remember falling asleep. The last thing I remembered was reading my dad's letter and touching that blue disc.

The disc! The minute I realized it wasn't in my hand, I felt a surge of panic. Where was it? I glanced around the room. It was gone.

I dove for my father's letter, still lying on my bed, and riffled through the pages. No disc. I turned the yellow envelope upside down. Nothing. Then I dropped to the floor and crawled under the bed on my hands and knees. When I found nothing there, not even the slightest speck of dirt by the way, I leapt to my feet and tore the sheets and blankets from the bed and shook them wildly in the air. Dmitri just stood there, staring at me with his beady eyes.

"Dmitri, could you just give me a little space? I lost something I need to find, okay?" I was beginning to feel a dread rising in me.

"Are you looking for that CD?"

I whipped around and stared at him. "Where is it?"

"I put it on the desk."

"Well, thanks for telling me, Dmitri."

"You're welcome, Leo."

Apparently, my sarcasm was lost on him.

I took the yellow envelope over to the desk, pushed the disc inside, and sealed the flap shut. Although a great feeling of relief swept over me, I did my best to hide it from Dmitri. I didn't want him to know how important that disc was to me. I didn't even understand it myself. All I knew was that I wanted the disc someplace where that kid couldn't find it.

"Dmitri," I said in my nicest voice. "Could you wait outside for a minute? I have to change my shirt."

"It's just your stomach. You don't have to be ashamed in front of me. We're friends."

"I don't know how to break it to you, man, but we just met."

"Okay, okay. I'll wait outside." He walked over to me, patted me on the back for some reason, and then left.

Alone in the room, I folded my dad's letter carefully, put it back in the envelope with the blue disc, and slid the package under my mattress. I hurriedly put on a new shirt, which was actually dirtier than the first one. As I pulled the shirt over my ears, I became aware of a strange melody playing softly in my head. Perhaps it had been there all along and it was the silence that made me notice it.

What was that song? What was going on with me? I reassured myself that I was exhausted and your mind does strange things when you're really tired. And that I had actually fallen asleep on the floor, just like I told Dmitri.

But inside, I knew that wasn't true.

I found Dmitri squatting against the wall in the corridor. Hollis's door was open, and I heard the sound of a TV. He was lying in bed, watching a large television that seemed to be made out of the same material as the wall.

"TV sucks on Sunday," he said. "Nothing on but old guys talking about the news."

"At least you have a TV," I answered. "I don't."

"Yes you do, ding-dong. The control panel is in the wall next to your bed. Push the red button — that gets you to the entertainment menu screen, then it's just a few more commands until a TV opens up from the wall. How cool is that?"

Dmitri wandered in, even though no one had invited him, and made himself right at home in front of Hollis's TV.

"The black button opens the closet," he explained, "and the blue button turns on the shower in your bathroom. You use the number pad to call me or my father."

The control panel was like a computer touch screen. Hollis entered a few commands and the TV switched to an old submarine movie.

"Leave it," I commanded. "This is the one where they mistake the humpback whale for a Russian sub. I love this movie."

Dmitri pushed another button on the control panel, and the TV clicked off.

"Hey, who said you could do that?" Hollis barked.

Hollis was never much on politeness and good manners. But Dmitri didn't seem to mind. He seemed like one of those kids who hangs around, no matter what.

"It is time for lunch," he simply said. "My *matka* has been cooking all day and there is a birthday cake for Leo."

"Like we even know what a *matka* is," Hollis snorted.

"You eat them on Hanukkah, dummy," I said.

"*Matka* is Polish for mother," Dmitri cut in. "Matka is *my* mother. She cooks for Crane."

"What is it exactly that your father does for Uncle Crane?" I asked him.

Dmitri didn't answer, just smiled this weird little smile. Then he said, "My father taught me to work all the machines in Crane's business. Come here, feel my muscle."

He flexed his biceps, and I saw that he definitely had man muscles. I'd been waiting for mine to pop out for a while now. I know it's all supposed to happen at once . . . growth spurt, puberty, man muscles, facial hair . . . but so far, even though I'm thirteen, I have nothing to show in any of those departments. Zip. Zilch. Nada.

Dmitri's invitation to feel his muscles got Hollis out of bed, and fast. In a split second, he was running down the hall toward the dining room. I followed him, until we both realized that we hadn't seen a dining room anywhere in the apartment. Maybe Crane ate in the dugout canoe suspended from the ceiling. He'd have a good view, at least.

We didn't eat in the dugout canoe, but we did eat in someplace almost as weird. Uncle Crane was waiting for us in a totally empty room next to the elevator. When we arrived, he put an arm around each of us and walked us over to a control panel on the wall.

"Who wants to push the T button and see what happens?" he asked. He seemed really tickled with himself.

Hollis blocked me with his body and pushed the button. There was a little whir, then a table made of shiny silver metal descended from the ceiling. No kidding, it looked like a spaceship landing.

"Wow," Hollis said. "Wait till I tell my friends about this."

"Is there a C button I can push to get the chairs?" I asked Crane.

"In this household, Leo, we don't use chairs."

"What do we use? Cushions, stools, couches?"

"None of the above, my dear Leo. We eat standing up. In this way, we consume smaller portions and we burn calories as we eat. Americans spend entirely too much time lolling about a table, getting fat. I have no patience for that custom."

Olga brought out a few small plates of food and we stood at the table eating. I could have used a whole lot more food, but I knew not to ask for more. I certainly didn't want any more criticism of my cheeks. Standing there with Uncle Crane made me miss our dinner table at home, where my mom put big platters of food in the middle of the table, and we all just helped ourselves and had a good time.

As we ate, Klevko and Dmitri kept coming into the room and skulking around, always hovering over my shoulder. At the end of the meal, which didn't take more than five minutes to finish, Klevko brought out a brownish birthday cake with mustard-yellow icing. There was only one candle instead of thirteen. I hoped it was one of those trick candles that don't go out no matter how hard you blow, but it wasn't. Of course it wasn't. Uncle Crane wasn't the kind of guy who'd get a big hoot out of trick candles. Anyway, he left to take a business call before the cake was even served. We could hear him talking on the phone in a language that sounded Russian. At least I think it was Russian, because he sounded like those guys on the submarine in the movie.

After lunch and the non-celebration birthday celebration, I asked Uncle Crane if we could see the rest of the building.

"There are six floors below us filled with the pieces I buy and sell," he said. "But they are all crated up, so there is not much to see."

"How much are all those *artifacts* worth?" Hollis asked.

"I like your thinking, Hollis, but it's better you don't know. I don't want you boys to be tempted to tell any of your school chums about our warehouse and its contents. We are here in this sorry salami district of Brooklyn precisely so no one will suspect the wealth I have accumulated here."

After a little begging on Hollis's part, Uncle Crane agreed to show us one of the lower floors of the warehouse. He took us in the elevator and we went down to the third floor. Of course, Klevko accompanied us. He seemed to shadow Uncle Crane everywhere he went.

When the elevator opened onto the third floor, all we saw were rows and rows of crates and boxes and bins, each labeled in black stencil with a long number. Uncle Crane was right. There wasn't much to see.

"Do you actually know what's in all of these?" I asked him.

"Each and every one, Leo. I acquired each piece with great care. These boxes are like my children." Crane ran his veiny hand along the top of one.

Hollis peeked through the wooden slats of one of the crates, then jumped about ten feet in the air.

"There's a T. rex in there, I swear."

"That is the skull of a carnivorous dinosaur that I acquired from a collector in Marrakesh," Uncle Crane said proudly.

"A real T. rex? Shouldn't a thing like that be in a museum?" I asked.

Crane reached out and pinched my cheek. I'll be honest, I wasn't loving this cheek-pinching thing.

"It will be, Leo. I have several natural history museums bidding against each other as we speak. Oh, how I love the business of business."

Hollis was already looking into another crate, this one farther down the row. Klevko was circling around him, keeping watch.

"In that container, my dear Hollis, is a thirty-six-million-year-old fossilized penguin."

"That is completely weird and cool all at the same time," Hollis said. I was waiting for him to ask how much it was worth.

"Penguins don't go back thirty-six million years," I said. When I was a kid, I was really into dinosaurs, and I wanted to let Crane know that I knew a thing or two about fossils. But apparently, not as much as I thought.

"Leo, your ignorance is showing," Crane said, shaking a manicured index finger at me. "This fossil of the *Inkayacu paracasensis*, or water king, dates from the Eocene period and was found just recently in Peru. The bird stood nearly five feet tall, and was twice the weight of today's emperor penguin. It will do you well, young Leo, not to question my expertise again."

What could I say to that? Nothing, except excuse me for being such a dummy. And I wasn't about to give him the satisfaction of saying that. Fortunately, Hollis jumped in.

"So, Uncle Crane, how do you get this stuff?" he asked.

"I have my ways. And trust me, they are very effective."

"Yes, boss, I remember when we got that penguin," Klevko said, letting loose one of his gargle-laughs. "That night on the wharf with those two South American guys with machetes and the police officer who—"

"That's enough, Klevko," Crane said with an unsmiling look. "You don't have to tell everything you know."

Crane walked down the row and stopped at a huge crate. It was easily the size of a car.

"Here's something you will like, boys. It is a ten-foot-long tusk of a woolly mammoth found on the Siberian tundra. A rare artifact indeed."

"How much is that worth?" Hollis the money-grubber asked.

"On a good day, a million dollars."

Hollis's eyes nearly rolled back in his head. "That's a lot of moolah," he said. "You could buy a yacht with that."

"Can we see the tusk?" I asked.

"I suppose a quick glance wouldn't hurt. Klevko, a little help here."

Klevko slid the top of the crate off just enough so we could see in. Crane wasn't kidding—that tusk really was ten feet long, with a sharp point at the end. I reached out and ran my hand along the smooth white ivory. All of a sudden, I started to feel dizzy. To steady myself, I grabbed on to the curve of the tusk. I could have sworn I heard a sound, like the muffled trumpet of an elephant. Worried that I might pass out, I let go of the tusk and put my head between my knees.

"Leo, are you unwell?" Uncle Crane asked.

"Just feeling a little dizzy."

"Of course you are, Leo. You've had a terrible trauma, and I'm sure this move isn't easy for you. What you need is rest. I suggest you boys go to your rooms and relax. Tomorrow you're back to school, and you'll need your strength."

We rode back up to the penthouse in the elevator, and by the time we were at the apartment, the dizzy feeling and the trumpeting sound had gone away. Uncle Crane told us he had a business meeting with some Russians that evening, so we spent the rest of the night lying on the floor in Hollis's room watching television. If we got hungry, all we had to do was buzz the control panel and either Klevko or Dmitri would bring us snacks.

Trevor texted me twice and called to wish me a happy birthday, but I didn't feel like calling him back. I had seen him two or three times since the plane crash, and I could tell he felt bad for me but didn't know what to say. When you think about it, what was there to say? *"I'm sorry your parents are dead?"*

Yeah, me too. Big time.

At ten o'clock, I got up to go to my room, but Hollis pulled me back.

"Leo," he said. "Do you think everyone's going to come up to us at school tomorrow and say how sorry they are?"

"I don't know. I hope not."

"Me too, because if they do and if I cry, I'm going to be really embarrassed. It's so uncool to cry in front of girls."

"Actually, Hollis, I'm told they kind of like it. Shows you're a sensitive guy and all."

I was just saying that to make him feel better. The truth is, I don't know a thing about what girls like or don't like, having had next to no experience in the boy-girl thing. I have friends who are girls, but I've never actually had a girlfriend. That's Hollis's area — he's the popular Lomax. All the girls in his grade think he's good-looking, with his shiny black hair like our mom's — not all brown and lumpy like mine. Girls love it that he's really musical and plays a great guitar and is an excellent dancer. Not like me, who walks around with a tape recorder picking up the sound of mosquitoes buzzing and cement mixers cranking. I haven't found a girl yet who wants to listen to the sound of a dump truck downshifting. Maybe someday I will, though.

Hollis got in bed and I tossed him his stuffed elephant, which had fallen on the floor.

"Here you go, chief. Trunkie doesn't mind if you cry."

I got up and went into my room, and as I did so, I heard Hollis turn on one of my mom's CDs. I knew I should try to get some sleep so I could get up in the morning for school. I reached over to the control panel and flicked off the lights. I had turned thirteen that day, but I wished this spaceship room had a night-light. As I lay there in the dark, the memory of my dad's letter came back to me. I couldn't shut out all those confusing images of that island, those people, the holy man in yellow. Dad had promised that telling me about my birth would give me insight into who I was. But it was the opposite. I had so many questions to ask, and no way to reach him. Maybe there were answers on that blue disc. I needed answers. I was having too many weird feelings to ignore.

At some point I fell asleep, though I don't remember how long I lay there in the darkness imagining the faraway island and listening to the half-remembered song that played over and over again in my head.

CHAPTER 5

woke up to the sound of heavy footsteps running around my room. Rubbing the sleep from my eyes, I saw Klevko scurrying back and forth between my bed and the door, slapping his chest with his hand.

"Leo, let's go, eh. Come, get up. Your uncle Crane, he's taking you boys to school. Time to get up like a man and study hard."

He ran out of my room and into Hollis's. Hollis groaned like he was being tortured and then I heard him shout, "Get outta here, I'm sleeping!"

Klevko trotted back into my room. "Your brother is so mean. He is like a sleeping bear." He started slapping his hands on his chest again. "You wake him. Come, get up."

I was about to tell Klevko no way, when I heard that thin, lizardy voice coming down the hallway.

"Arise, gentlemen," Uncle Crane called. "Time to make use of your day."

He appeared at the door of my room, wearing a beige turtleneck and green sport coat, perfectly dressed. I'd say that there wasn't a hair out of place, except Crane didn't have any hair, just a shiny bald head that glistened like gold. I thought of my dad who used to shuffle around in his old slippers every morning, his old blue robe thrown over his saggy pajamas, and wondered how two members of the same family could be so different.

"My friend Klevko the donkey has gotten you up late," Crane said. Klevko looked hurt. "Oh, Klevko, don't sulk. You know I love you. Now hurry, boys, your education will not wait."

"I'm up, Uncle Crane!" I heard Hollis shout. Normally, it was impossible to get that kid out of bed, so I knew he was trying hard to make an impression. Hollis cared a lot about what Crane thought of him. Me, I couldn't care less.

"I like your zest, Hollis," Crane said. "Now go help your slacker brother put on fresh slacks."

I didn't wait for Hollis to help me with my slacks since I didn't even own a pair of slacks, and if I did, I certainly wasn't about to wear them to school. But I had my backpack ready, jeans on, and teeth brushed inside of four minutes. I was going so quickly that I didn't think about how much I didn't want to go to school, just that I had to get there. Right before leaving, I remembered the disc, and slipped the yellow envelope into my backpack.

I had plans for that disc.

I met Hollis in the hall and together we half jogged through the rooms of swords and masks and statues and bridges. When we got to the elevator, Crane and Klevko were waiting.

"Three and a half minutes late," Crane said, tapping his watch.

As he ushered us into the elevator, Crane looked at me and raised an eyebrow. From his look, I thought maybe I had a huge blob of ketchup on my shirt or something really gross. I looked down but everything looked cool to me. Crane shook his head and, without a word, picked a tiny piece of lint off my shirt, then brushed the fabric hard. Wow, did that ever make me feel like a total loser slob.

Klevko slid the bronze gate closed with a rattle and yanked on the lever. With a grinding noise, the elevator shot up.

Up? Why up? The street wasn't up. It was down. What was going on?

The elevator lurched to a stop and opened into the hazy morning light. We were on the roof. A loud whirring noise surrounded us and gusts of wind blew dust and garbage around our feet like swirling little tornadoes. Crane put his hands on our shoulders and guided us around a corner. A jet-black helicopter, blades spinning, was getting ready for takeoff.

"No way," Hollis said.

"Why walk when you can fly?" Uncle Crane answered.

Hollis and I just looked at each other and grinned.

"Heads down, boys," Crane warned, guiding us over to the helicopter. We climbed in through the open door, where a pilot was sitting at the controls. Before I even put my safety straps on, we were lifting off. We hovered a thousand feet above the East River, then turned and headed toward Manhattan.

"Is this your helicopter?" I shouted at Uncle Crane, who was sitting in front next to the pilot.

"I own a share of it," Crane shouted back. "And a share of a private jet, too."

I tried to ask more, but it was useless, because the chopper noise was so loud, I couldn't hear a thing. So I just sat back, enjoyed the amazing ride, and tried not to barf on the back of the pilot's head.

The helicopter flew along the river toward uptown where our school is located. From that altitude, all the waves in the water below looked frozen, like blue sand dunes. I wondered if being seen arriving at school in a helicopter was a good thing or a bad thing. I knew Hollis would love it. He has a ton of friends and likes to be the center of attention. I tend to be shy and hang out mostly with Trevor, so for me, landing in a helicopter would probably be pretty embarrassing.

"Park it over there," Crane shouted at the pilot, pointing to a huge green circle with an *H* in the middle of it, located on top of a tall office building. "It's as close as we're going to get."

As the helicopter crossed over Central Park and then began its descent, the inside shook so much it felt like it was going to break apart. I didn't want to show how scared I was, so I started humming real loud. *Hmmmmmmmmmmmmmmm.* The rotating blades made my voice all shaky like when you talk into a fan. Hollis started humming, too, and I pulled out my mini recorder in time to catch a little of our vibrating voices before we touched down. It was such an interesting sound that, for once, Hollis didn't make fun of me recording it.

After we landed, Crane hurried us into a stairwell on the roof, which led us to the top floor of the building. Hollis was buzzed and couldn't stop asking questions.

"Can we take the chopper again tomorrow, Uncle Crane? Can I pilot it? Will it pick us up after school?"

"This won't be a daily occurrence, Hollis, but since I was going to New Jersey anyway, I thought you boys might enjoy it. I have arranged for Stump to pick you up after school."

"That's okay, Uncle Crane," I said. "I'm going to Jeremy's. I'll take the subway home. I have a MetroCard."

"And who exactly is Jeremy?"

"Jeremy Sebold. He's my tutor. He was one of my dad's graduate students."

"Ah yes, I remember now. Your father left instructions in his will. This person is to guide your education in special projects, correct?"

"He's a great guy."

"This supposed great guy owns some kind of music establishment in Harlem, correct?"

"Yeah, he runs a used-record store. He's a collector and has every kind of music you can think of. I hang out there a lot."

"It figures that your father would befriend a person like that. It sounds like a colossal waste of time to me, but if it's what your father wanted, then I suppose I can't say no. What about you, Hollis?"

"Will Stump have the limo?" he asked.

"Yes, of course."

"Awesome. Then I'll go home with him."

"Very good, Hollis."

I flinched when I heard Hollis say the word *home*. Had he forgotten our real home so quickly? I would never feel at home in Crane's apartment, not ever.

"Now, gentlemen, you are three blocks from school and thirty flights from the street," Crane said, tapping his watch, a habit of his I was already starting to dislike. "Take the elevator down and then run like the dickens. You have five minutes to get to school."

It sure wasn't the way our mom used to send us off to school in the morning. There was no "good-bye," no "have a nice day," no "be sure to eat something green at lunch." Just a quick pivot and he was gone into the stairwell and his waiting helicopter.

Actually, we only had four minutes. It was 8:26 and school started at 8:30, so we did exactly what Uncle Crane told us to do, ran like the dickens.

Our school, the Academy of Sciences and Arts, goes all the way from kindergarten to twelfth grade. Hollis and I are both at the middle school campus on 95th street — he's in sixth grade and I'm in seventh. In September, when he first came up from the elementary school, I was really annoyed to have him around because he was everything that I wasn't. He was popular, he was a good soccer player, and he played lead guitar in a kid garage band. Hollis can play anything . . . guitar, piano, drums, even the saxophone. Mostly I hang out with Trevor and a few other science guys at school, and even though kids generally like me, I'm just not a people magnet like Hollis is. My dad always said the most important thing is to be who you are, and the right people will find you. I was counting on that being true.

We made it up the school steps just before the bell rang. We pushed open the main door, and as I stood there catching my breath, it gave me a chance to notice all the kids standing around talking and laughing. It struck me how much their lives hadn't changed while mine was turned totally upside down. Hollis was immediately surrounded by a bunch of his friends. Lauren Rollins gave him half of her blueberry muffin. Samir Joshi handed him copies of all his homework assignments, which he had put in a folder for him. Aaron Hartley invited him to sleep over after soccer practice. Hollis glanced over at me, smiling.

"I'm going to be okay, bro. You all right?"

"Sure, I'll be fine. See ya later, chief."

Hollis went off with his friends and I headed upstairs for homeroom. As I reached the second floor, I saw Trevor sprinting down the hall toward me. He's in Ms. Navarro's homeroom next door to mine. Trevor's easy to pick out in a crowd because he's at least six inches taller than every other kid. When we were younger, coaches always wanted him to try out for the basketball team. Trevor's dad told them that just because he's African-American and tall is no reason he has to like basketball. So he became a science whiz instead. He loves all science, but especially mechanical stuff. He can fix anything because he understands the principles of how things work. His dad, who installs heating and air-conditioning units in all the big apartments in New York, taught him how to use tools when he was practically a baby. Not my dad. He taught me how to listen to sounds. We all have our special skills, I guess.

"Hey, Leo, good to see you back," Trevor said, holding up his hand for a high five. "Even though you don't return my texts."

We were outside the door to my homeroom, where Madison McAndrews was about to go in. She was a brainiac, winner of the Math Olympiad last year.

"Oh, Leo, I'm so sorry to hear about your mom and dad." She reached out and put a hand on my shoulder. Madison McAndrews had never even looked at me before, let alone touched me. "Maybe we can hang out sometime," she added. "Do some algebra or something."

I felt tears starting to well up, but I tried desperately not to look as sad as I felt. I knew she was feeling sorry for me, and the last thing I wanted to look was pathetic.

"Sounds good," I said, trying to plaster on a chipper smile. "I'm never one to turn down help with my linear equations."

Mr. Judd, my homeroom teacher, stuck his head out into the hall.

"Leo, are you planning to join us?"

Good old Mr. Judd. He would never be nice, not even to a kid in my situation. Actually, I appreciated him acting normal to me and not all warm and fuzzy.

"When can we talk?" I whispered to Trevor.

"Meet me in the library at lunch," he said. "Science and technology section."

I had so much to tell him — about Crane's warehouse full of stuff, my crazy spaceship bedroom, and my helicopter ride to school. I wasn't planning to tell him about the letter from my dad or the blue disc. My dad had specifically said to keep it a secret. The only person I was planning to tell about the disc was Jeremy because he could help me find a way to play it.

I got through the morning better than I expected. I was actually relieved to be back at school and have my teachers' voices filling my head rather than those other strange sounds that I had experienced — the elephant trumpeting, the crashing waves, the strange haunting melody. Most people at school made special attempts to be extra nice to me. The school counselor, Mrs. King, brought me a hot chocolate at snack time and told me I could talk to her anytime, about anything. Anything at all.

I got in line and bought a chicken sandwich from the cafeteria, wolfing it down as I hurried to the library to meet Trevor. On the way in, I crashed smack into a girl on her way out of the library. Not just any girl, but the most gorgeous girl in the seventh grade, Abby Two. That's not actually her name, but she came into our grade last year and there was already an Abby in our class so she just became known as Abby Two.

"Oh wow. I'm really sorry," I stammered. I had knocked her backpack to the floor, and a bunch of pens and pencils had fallen out and rolled away.

"Not your fault," Abby Two said, bending down to scoop up the pencils.

Trevor came over to help me recover from being such a clod. "Leo, you move just like a dancer."

Abby laughed. I saw one of her pens, a fancy black one with silver trim, had rolled under a bookshelf. I bent down to pick it up. It was the least I could do.

As I held the pen in my hand, my head started to spin with that same dizzy feeling I had in Crane's warehouse when I touched the mammoth tusk. Oh great. I hoped I wasn't going to puke right there in front of the most beautiful girl in the world. Breathe, Leo. As I took a deep breath, I thought I heard a man's voice way in the distance saying, "Merry Christmas, honey." I turned my head around to see who was talking but no one was.

Eager to get out of there before I actually did barf, I quickly handed the pen back to Abby. As soon as the pen left my hand, the dizzy feeling went away.

"Thanks, Leo," she said. "I'm so glad you found this one."

"Me too," I said. "You don't want to lose a present from your dad."

I don't know why I said that. It just came out of my mouth before I could stop myself. Abby looked at me in disbelief.

"How did you know?" she asked.

I shrugged. "I just had a feeling. Seems like a father-daughter special kind of gift thing."

She smiled at me and gave me a hug. That's right. An actual hug.

"You're such a sensitive person, to be able to feel that," she said, putting the pen in her backpack. "That's really cool. See you in Spanish, Leo."

Wow. Abby Two wanted to see me in Spanish. That was a first.

Trevor was eyeing me suspiciously.

"Pretty smooth, Leo. How'd you do it?"

"Do what?"

"You know, figure out that pen was a present from her dad."

I couldn't tell Trevor about the voice in my head. He'd think I was totally bonkers, which by the way, I was beginning to think myself.

"It's very logical, really," I stammered. "It was expensive so I guessed it was from one of her parents. That leaves either her mom or her dad. I had a fifty-fifty shot."

Trevor nodded.

He seemed satisfied with my explanation. It made sense. I wondered what he would say if I told him the truth — that a man's voice inside my head spoke to me from far away.

That thought made even *me* shudder.

CHAPTER 6

After school, Trevor caught up with me as I headed to the subway stop on Broadway. I was a man on a mission.

"You going to Jeremy's today?" he asked, falling in step with me.

I nodded.

"Great, I'm coming with you."

I was planning to talk only with Jeremy about the blue disc. I had to listen to my dad's instructions, and until I figured out a lot of things, I was on my own.

"Trev, I just want to walk there by myself. Do some thinking, okay?"

"Not okay, Leezer," he said, looking up just in time to avoid colliding with an oncoming woman pushing a stroller. "You need to be with people."

I smiled. My dad used to call me Leezer, and Trevor had adopted the nickname. He's the only person beside my dad who has a nickname for me—unless you want to count Hollis, who calls me Meathead.

"I know what you must be feeling, man," Trevor said.

I tried to laugh it off. "Since when did you get so sensitive anyway? Did you order a heart on eBay?"

"I read a pamphlet about the grieving process."

"Oh, so that's it. You almost sounded like a human there, for a minute."

"In computer science," Trevor said, "they say that if you can't tell the difference between a computer and a human, then they're both humans. You know, the Turing test."

Trevor is so smart that sometimes the things he says go right over my head. He thinks I'm smart, too, but I sure can't take apart a circuit board or spout off about electromagnetic flux like he can. But I make him think. Usually about crazy stuff, but what isn't?

The wind was blowing cold as we hurried down the street, so it was a relief to go down the stairs into the subway station where at least it wasn't totally freezing. My ears were so cold that I felt like they would break off if someone gave them a hard flick of the finger. I couldn't find my old hat anywhere this morning. Probably in some unmarked box with the rest of my parents' things.

Trevor and I swiped our MetroCards and headed for our platform. We'd been allowed to take the subway alone for two years now, and between us, we can get anywhere in the city we need to go.

We stood on the platform and waited for the 1 train that would take us up to Harlem. Nearby, a guy was playing a steel drum and the tinny sound of it echoing off the tile walls was like a metallic Ping-Pong ball. I thought about recording it, but decided against it since I had already made about twenty other steel drum recordings in various subway stops.

"So tell me again, Leezer, why were you taking a helicopter to school?" Trevor said, peering down at a huge rat sliding under the third rail.

"My uncle was going to meet a guy about buying a mummy. Or selling a mummy, I don't know which. He flies all over the world buying and selling really expensive old stuff."

"He must be one rich man to have his own chopper."

"He owns part of a private jet, too."

"Excellent. Be nice to the guy so we can go someplace on it. I'm up for Hawaii. Tahiti would work. Maybe you can invite Abby Two. She likes you, after that psychic brain demonstration."

I knew Trevor was just joking about my psychic brain, but I truly believed something had spoken to me during that moment with Abby. I was afraid to even consider what it was.

Our train arrived, and we hopped on. The car was relatively empty, which is to say no one was standing up except one old woman with no front teeth and a plastic bag on her head, who looked at me and said, "I am the Queen of All Things and you are my loyal subject." She also proclaimed this to the three other people who got on with us. No one seemed to mind.

Trevor and I found two seats together and sat down. As the train lurched forward, I thought I'd try to bring up the subject of those sounds in my head, but in a roundabout way, just to test the waters.

"Hey, Trev," I said hesitantly. "What do you think about mind reading, telepathy, stuff like that?"

"Extraordinary claims call for extraordinary evidence."

"Huh?"

"It's like this, Leez. If some guy told me that he boarded a flying saucer, before I'd believe his account, I'd have to see several high-quality photos, a radar blip, maybe even a piece of the saucer. He'd also have to tell me something completely new. Something nontrivial we don't know already. I'm open to anything, but I'd need a ton of unquestionable evidence, you know?"

"Okay, but what if it were someone you knew really well, someone like me, someone you trusted. Let's say I told you that last night I got beamed up to the mother ship, would you believe me?"

"Did you?"

"No, but what if I told you that?"

Trevor bit his lip.

"I'd have to think about that," he said after a moment. "But there'd probably be a rational explanation," he added quickly.

I wondered what Trevor would think if I told him I heard a man's distant voice in the school library, or that I was hearing ocean waves washing on the shore when I was in my room. Was that good enough evidence? Evidence of what? That I'd gone off the deep end? I'd never know unless I told him the truth, but somehow the subway didn't seem the right place. Besides, the Queen of All Things was already consuming all the crazy space in the car.

Jeremy's shop is on 128th, just a few blocks from the subway station. We went inside where it was warm and bright. Like always, the first thing that hit me when I walked in was the music and the speakers buzzing. Jeremy is usually playing weird music that sounds like farm animals being tickled. But this day, he was playing harp music, and it made me imagine this mermaid on the rocks. It was pretty relaxing.

"Yo, Jeremy, it's me," I hollered.

There wasn't much need to yell. The shop is very small. It's crammed to the ceiling with records — stacked in boxes, filed in bins, leaned up against walls, big ones and little ones, strewn everywhere among countless scraps of paper and posters of musical greats. This was my dad's favorite place in the whole world.

From behind his rickety wooden desk, Jeremy saw us come in, but he was on the phone. He cupped the receiver and mouthed, "Just a sec." Surrounded by all his equipment and crazy stacks of records, he looked like a mad scientist busy at his workbench. Jeremy's rumpled, mismatched clothes reminded me of my dad. No wonder they were such good friends. That and the fact that they both loved music more than anything in the world.

While we were waiting, Trevor and I flipped through some of the bins. I found this one bizarre record called *Fresh*

Metzger. The cover was of this bearded guy's face that was being sprayed by the shower, and his huge, gross beard was dripping water. Just as I was about to show it to Trevor, I smelled something pretty foul, yet familiar, approaching from behind me.

"Hey, Leo."

I spun around, my nose tingling and twitching. It was Stinky Steve. He works for Jeremy a couple days a week, and yes, he always smells. He was wearing short shorts even though it was January, and bizarre rust-colored jogging shoes. And as always, he was wearing his fanny pack.

"Hey, Steve. How's it going?"

I looked around for Trevor, who had conveniently disappeared behind a column when he saw Steve coming. I needed backup. Conversations with Stinky Steve are generally long, boring, and strange.

"Things are rocking here, dude. A customer brought in a collection to sell, mostly common major label rock from the '60s, so I bought it all for cheap, you know, just for store stock. But when I examined the matrix numbers on the run-out groove, I saw that all the Capitols were pressed at the Scranton plant, which meant that they were all the special masters by the great Wally Traugot, the hot stampers, you know? I did a side-by-side comparison and . . ."

Stinky Steve was the ultimate record nerd, and I couldn't take another minute of it. I caught Trevor peeking out from behind the column.

"Steve," I interrupted, "did you see that Trevor's here?"

"Hey, Trevor, do you like digital sound?" he asked. As always, Steve didn't wait for an answer. "If you ask me, digital sound is an abomination, the worst thing to happen to music since the Great Depression killed jazz, and World War II killed the 78 industry. And —"

"Success!" I heard Jeremy shout, slamming down the phone. He came out from behind his desk just in time to rescue us.

"Hey, Leo. Hey, Trevor, long time no see. Come into my office."

Of course, there was no office, but we went back to his desk, leaving Stinky Steve to continue his rant solo.

"Sorry about that, guys," Jeremy said. "I was on the phone with this musician's family. This guy made one amazing album in 1968. And he only made twelve copies of it. I've been trying to track him down for ten years. About five years ago, I learned that he was in a mental institution, and had made the album there. Then the trail ran dry. But I finally got hold of his family, and they have more copies of the record. Records!"

"Records!" Stinky Steve screamed from across the shop.

"You want a record made by a crazy guy?" Trevor asked.

"You bet," Jeremy said. "Real music by real people."

I had often heard my dad say that same sentence. He said aside from me and Hollis and my mom, it was the most important thing to him, to record real music made by real people.

"So how's it going with the stepuncle, Leo? What's he like?" Jeremy asked, brushing some long strands of hair away and looking for a new record to put on. Even though he was just in his late twenties, Jeremy had some gray in his shaggy beard and scruffy ponytail.

"He's got his own helicopter and is filthy rich," Trevor chimed in.

"No wonder Kirk left you and Hollis in his care." Jeremy nodded. "You guys won't need a thing. Your dad thought of everything, Leo. He was one in a million."

"He left me something that I want you to see," I said quietly to Jeremy. "Is there someplace private we can go?"

"I'd say sure, Leo, but the back room is filled up with a new collection, and the bathroom — er, let's just say Steve broke it. But you can tell me here, just us boys."

I hesitated and looked over at Trevor.

"Hey, Trev," I whispered. "Do you mind if I talk to Jeremy alone for a sec?" Trevor and I had never had any secrets from each other, so he looked a little confused. "Just some stuff about my dad," I added. "It's kind of private."

Trevor saw the look on my face and understood.

"I'll step over there and continue my discussion with Steve," he said. "You guys can talk. Maybe the stench of his body odor will clear my sinuses." I decided then that when I knew more, so would he. I couldn't lie to him much longer.

I pulled the yellow envelope from my backpack and carefully slid the blue disc onto the desk. Jeremy looked at it and whistled softly.

"There's an oldie," he said.

"I found this in one of my dad's old boxes. I think it's a record, but I've never seen one like it."

"It's a record, definitely. But you're right, it's unique. So unique you can't play it on a normal turntable."

"Why not?"

Jeremy picked up the blue disc and turned it over delicately in his fingertips.

"This is a recordable disc they used to make in the nineteen fifties for a device called an Audograph. They only made them for a few years. You talked into it, and it actually made its own little records, like this one."

"Why'd they stop making them?"

"They were used mostly by secretaries, to record dictation from their bosses. When more portable devices came along, like tape recorders, the Audograph died out. Leave it to Kirk to pick the most obscure way to record whatever is on that disc."

"I need to get hold of an Audograph to play it."

"Good luck, Lomax. Those things are impossible to find."

"Can we at least try it on your record player?" I asked. I could hear the desperation in my voice. I had to know what was on that disc.

"We might hear something, but we'd probably ruin the thing. You need to find an original machine, but they're as rare as hens' teeth."

Suddenly, I felt a large presence over my shoulder, and smelled that special aroma that only Stinky Steve emits.

"Couldn't help overhearing," he wheezed. "Is that an Audograph disc you got there? I have a whole collection of those. The rarest ones are the blue color you have, the less rare ones are red and green. It's pretty fun to listen to them. Mostly just boring office stuff, but I like to hear how normal people talked back in the nineteen fifties."

"What do you listen to them on?" I asked him.

"I have an Audograph player. Bought it off King George at the East Village flea market. Paid seventy-five bucks and the damn thing didn't work. Wouldn't even power up. I went back to King George and told him I wanted my money back—"

"Does it work now?" I interrupted.

"It didn't for a long time, Leo. I had to special order these tiny screws from a store in Florida. I went all over the city looking for those buggers. I went downtown and uptown, even took the ferry out to Staten Island. Finally, I found that place in Florida. They charged me seven dollars and ninety-five cents for screws, for *screws*. Can you believe it?"

By now, Trevor had wandered over and was listening to the conversation. So much for my privacy. I might as well have stood on the top of the Empire State Building and told the world I had a secret disc from my dad.

"Steve," I said, "this is really important. Could you bring the machine over so I can listen to this disc?"

"No way. It's fragile, dude. Held together with cheap tiny screws, screws that cost me seven dollars and ninety-five cents, *plus* shipping. Seven dollars and ninety-five cents for some screws! Besides, Mama's probably asleep, and I can't wake her before *Jeopardy!* time."

I couldn't take it anymore. I was this close to hearing what could be the most important information of my life, but I couldn't get there because of some crazy old lady's TV-watching schedule.

"Can you help me out here?" I practically begged Jeremy. "I have got to hear this disc." Jeremy scratched his beard, thought for a second, then nodded.

"Steve," he said. "I happen to have just found a *Relatively Clean Rivers* record that I *was* holding for —"

"Not the original pressing, right?" Steve asked, his eyes bugging out of his head. He was almost drooling.

"Original pressing." Jeremy winked at me. "If you could find a way to let Leo use your Audograph, that record is yours. Oh, and it's still sealed."

"No way. In that case, no problem." Steve turned to me. "You can come up to my apartment and listen to it there. Whatever you need, Leo. Your friend can come, too."

"He has to get home," I said.

"And leave you with this nutcase?" Trevor whispered. "No way."

"Where exactly is your Audograph?" I asked Steve.

"In my room, with all my other vintage audio equipment. Wait till you see it all, dude. I've got a Marantz 2330b receiver from the seventies and a classic Linn Sondek turntable with an amazing Ittok LVII arm and a —"

"Steve, hold up. Listen, man, is there a door to your room? So I could have some privacy?"

"Sure, have all the privacy you want. Trevor and I can hang in the living room and watch *Jeopardy!* with Mama. What do you say, Trev?"

"Sure, but I'm warning you, I'll wipe the floor with you guys, *Jeopardy!*-wise."

"Oh, you haven't met Mama," Steve said.

It was settled. I threw on my jacket and headed for the door. I couldn't get to Steve's fast enough. As we left the shop, Jeremy called after me.

"Come back and tell me what's on that disc, Leo. I'm curious as hell. Bet you are, too."

Curious? Yeah, I was curious. I was also excited, nervous, nauseous, sweaty, jittery, worried, and totally terrified.

And that was just for starters.

CHAPTER 7

We left the shop and followed Steve to his apartment. All you had to do was follow the smell trail that Steve left behind. His apartment was above the 99 cent store, four flights up.

"You better listen fast, Leo," Trevor said as we climbed the narrow stairway. "I don't know how much *Jeopardy!* with Mama I can take."

Pulling out his key on a keychain that had about twenty-five other keys, Steve said to us, "Don't make any noise in there until we get to my room. Mama likes to rest her brain until *Jeopardy!* time."

"Naps are good for intelligence," Trevor said. "But for the best results, you shouldn't nap for more than an hour."

Good for Trevor, I thought. He could keep up with Steve fact for fact.

We went in. All the couches were covered with plastic and everywhere was that old-woman smell. Stinky Steve and his Equally Stinky Mama. The room we were in was like a giant display case. The walls were covered with plates, the kind you see on TV commercials that have pictures of presidents on them, the ones you can buy for "three easy payments of only $19.99." There must have been 300 spooky faces staring out at us — presidents, old actors and actresses, sports stars, and animals of all sorts. Anyone or anything that old people like, and they had a plate of it.

"These commemorative plates are Mama's pride and joy," Steve whispered. "The whole collection is worth over fifty thousand dollars."

"That's good, Steve, but if it's okay with you, can we just get to the Audograph?"

"This one is worth a fortune," he went on. "It's Annie Red, who was supposed to be a big movie star in the nineteen fifties but in the middle of her first movie, there was a terrible accident. It was supposed to take place in ancient Rome, and a tiger on set went nuts and clawed half her face off. She never acted again. Some people think she's still alive, living by herself, no guests and no mirrors."

Trevor and I glanced at each other. This guy was weirder than we'd thought. A shrill voice screeched through the walls.

"Stevie!" she called. "Who's there? What are you doing? What time is it? Bring me my slippers. Stevie!"

He turned to us and whispered, "Just a second. It's Mama."

When he was gone, Trevor nudged me in the arm. "These guys are like the zombies under the stairs. Straight out of a horror movie."

"Hey, be quiet for a second," I whispered. From the next room, you could hear Steve and his mom talking. I strained to hear. "I wonder what they're talking about."

"Which commemorative plates they're going to serve us on after they cook us," Trevor said. We both cracked up and hunched over holding our guts to try to stifle the laughs.

Ordinarily, Trevor and I would have done a whole comedy routine about the plates. But all I could think about was that disc. I was dying to hear what it had to tell me. When Steve came back into the living room, I almost pounced on him.

"Hey, Steve," I lied, "I just talked to Jeremy on the phone. He said he's closing up the shop early, so if you want the record today, we have to get back there soon."

"Then let's get on it, partner." Finally.

Steve showed us into his room, which was nothing like the main apartment. It was clean, organized, and packed with shelves and shelves of records and the coolest-looking stereo equipment ever. His bed was just a sad little cot in the corner.

"Here's the Audograph."

He pointed to a metal machine. It had some knobs like an old TV set, but other than its curvy shape, it didn't look like any record player that I'd seen. Steve uncoiled the microphone cable and the plug, and searched around for an empty jack.

"So this thing records sound?" I asked, not quite believing it.

"How does it work?" Trevor asked as Steve got to his hands and knees and crawled under the desk, looking for the jack. I'm not even going to mention the words *butt crack* here, but let's just say, his was getting some air.

"You guys know that the sound we hear is just waves?" Steve grunted as he stretched himself to the breaking point to reach the jack. "Well, sound is just waves. Waves are energy that travels outward, like what happens when you drop a rock in a pool of water. The sounds we hear are just what our brains make of the very fast sound waves vibrating the air around us. No air, no sound."

"Which is why you can't hear in space," Trevor said.

"Or how when you hear sound underwater, it's much higher pitched," I added.

"Whoa, you guys are smart," Steve grunted. "Almost there, just one last push."

Trevor put his face right up to the machine. I could tell that he would have liked nothing more than to rip the top off and poke around inside to see how it worked.

"Sound waves travel faster in water than in air, because water is denser," Steve droned on. "Every sound wave has a top and a bottom. The faster the top repeats, the higher pitched the sound is."

I could see Trevor taking down notes in his computer, I mean his brain, but I was almost unbearably impatient to hear my disc.

"Hey, Steve," I blurted out, unable to control myself any longer. "Not to be rude or anything, but could I try the Audograph now?"

"Sure, dude. It's almost time for *Jeopardy!* anyway."

Steve walked over to the Audograph. "So this is the machine," he said. "It has a little microphone. Your voice goes through some wires, and they convert your voice into electronic waves that make the Audograph's needle vibrate exactly like your voice. The needle etches all the sound waves of your voice onto the blank disc, and kind of makes a Jell-O mold out of them."

Steve flipped a switch, and the Audograph turned on with a low hum. "Takes a second for these old machines to power up. Where was I?"

"Jell-O mold," I said.

"Oh right. So after you record, you've got a disc with all the sound waves of your voice etched into it. Then when you play the disc, the needle runs through the grooves and vibrates against all the little notches in the material, and turns those into electrical signals. The signals run through some wires to turn the electronic waves into ones our ears can hear. And presto, you hear the sound come out of the speaker." Steve took a deep breath and scratched his protruding belly. "Easy, right?"

"Yup, pretty simple actually," Trevor said.

I didn't totally understand the rundown on the Audograph but at that point, I didn't care. My curiosity was not about the machine, but about the disc. The moment was here, and my hands were officially shaking. I pulled off my backpack and got to one knee. I slid the envelope up to the top of the bag, and just poked the top of the blue disc into the air.

"Can you put it on, Steve?" I asked. "I don't want to break it." I still wasn't sure what had happened yesterday when I touched the disc, but whatever it was, I didn't want it to happen again.

Steve cradled the slim disc in his fingertips, careful to a fault not to touch the middle part. He popped the disc into the Audograph. Then he twirled a few knobs and the machine started playing. I heard this low, scratchy sound coming out of the speaker.

"Wait!" I screamed. "Turn it off." Steve twirled a knob and the sound faded out with a warble.

"What's wrong, dude?"

"I'd like to listen to this by myself," I said. "I think it has an old family secret."

"I can relate. Mama and I, we have a few family secrets, too."

Behind Steve, I saw Trevor stifle a laugh and put his arms out in a zombie walk.

"I'll leave you alone," Steve said. "Slide this lever to 'play' to start it, and control the volume with the green knob. The needle goes from the inside to the outside, opposite of a regular record player. Just holler when you're done. Trevor, you ready for *Jeopardy?*"

"Born ready."

And with that, the two of them left me alone in Stinky Steve's room. I took a deep breath and turned the green knob.

CHAPTER 8

t was just me and the machine. I thought for a second how weird it was that I was about to discover the truth of who I am in some stranger's bedroom. It was weird, but it also felt right, because since I read my dad's letter, I had become a stranger to myself.

I sat down in front of the Audograph. I could hear the motor purring. Although the disc was spinning, I didn't hear anything, so I turned the volume up, all the way up.

A blast of static shot through the single speaker and jolted me upright. It sounded like a broom sweeping up piles of leaves, with tons of pops and clicks and crackles. As my ears adjusted to the static, I thought I heard the sound of the ocean in the background, muffled waves crashing in and getting sucked back out. Everything was tinny and distant, like the sound was being jammed through a pinhole.

Soon another sound emerged over the background of the ocean. It was somebody breathing, breathing very slowly at exactly the same pace as the tide. In and out. In and out. Could that be my dad breathing? On lots of my recordings, I can hear myself breathing.

I leaned toward the speaker, afraid that I might miss whatever was about to happen. A man's voice drifted in, half talking, half singing. At first I could barely make out his voice over the ocean and the static, but it got louder and louder until it was coming through clearly. I didn't understand the language, but the man was repeating many of the same words and phrases. I knew he was talking, but there was something singsong in his voice. When we studied Greek mythology in fifth grade, we learned about the ancient minstrels who would sing epic tales about heroes and legends, and I always imagined their voices would sound like that—quiet, steady, comforting, like a bedtime story.

Gradually the man's voice became more intense—he seemed almost possessed. I was sure this was the holy man, the shaman in yellow body paint and feathered headdress my dad described in his letter. My father had taught me a lot about shamans. In every group of people who don't have technology—and even in most that do—there's a shaman, a person who communicates with the spirit world. Besides the chief, he's the most important member of the group because he listens to the spirits who tell him the right path for his people to follow.

I could almost visualize the shaman as he chanted. His voice was powerful but delicate, like a large bird singing in the trees. He kept chanting the same melody, repeating it over and over so that I got caught up in the rhythm. I didn't notice that someone had started to play a type of drum under his chant — a big hollow sound that seemed to bend in the air.

The drumming was sparse at first, slow, with long stretches where the drummer was silent. Before I knew it, I found that I was swaying back and forth to this hypnotic rhythm. As the drum sped up, the shaman's voice became more urgent and powerful. A deep feeling of fright started to pool in my back, and I felt frozen, locked in their song.

Suddenly, out of nowhere, another voice came in, wailing in a high note that sounded like someone driving past in a fast car. Soon, several more men were singing with him in a chorus, all of their voices sliding wildly from high notes to low notes. The shaman was still chanting with the rhythm, a rhythm that seemed to match my own beating heart. I felt blood pulsing in my temples. The music was so beautiful and different from anything I had ever heard, and it was becoming all I was aware of.

And then I began to see things. The voices and sounds started to swirl into shapes of color in my mind. Each voice or instrument was a different color, and each moved just like its sound. The swirling lights were dim, like faint fireflies blinking on and off. I began to realize that I wasn't in Stinky Steve's room anymore, that I was somewhere else. Somewhere near the musicians. I could almost see them. A part of me was terrified. A part of me said, *Snap out of it.* But I couldn't move; I was paralyzed.

A chorus of women joined the men, singing in a round like "Row, Row, Row Your Boat," echoing the men's melody with their high, pure voices. Together it was all so beautiful. The shaman was still chanting underneath the music, but his voice seemed to reach out specifically to me, so that sometimes it was all I could hear.

The little fireflies of sound grew brighter now, multiplying so fast that they were everywhere. I suddenly felt I could see through the walls and had the feeling that I could travel through them, too, if I wanted. Something was waking up in me. Something I had secretly known about for a long time. Something that was familiar, but unknown — like the way you always have that same "feeling" right before you get sick. I wasn't sure if my eyes were open or closed.

The beautiful music was washing over me like waves. I felt like I was in warm ocean water, just relaxing in the tide as swirling colors of sound flickered in my eyes, almost too bright to look at. And then a wave of golden yellow crashed as a chorus of bamboo flutes joined their song. It was too much. So beautiful and moving that I was practically crying. I wanted to be there, on the beach next to those musicians, to be a part of their song. Suddenly, *I was there.* Suddenly, *I was one of them.* I saw the dark blue indigo sky and felt the heat of the sun. Then all the light melted away. I was alone. In darkness. I tried to wave my hand in front of my eyes, but I couldn't see anything. All I could hear was the slow crashing of waves. A tremendous calm came over me. Maybe I'm dead, I thought.

In the stillness, I heard the shaman's voice again, but he

wasn't chanting. He was singing, singing this unworldly melody from the back of his throat. Over and over he sang the same few words. The melody was far away yet all around me, the same half-forgotten melody that had been playing over and over in my head. But now I heard it all. It began to morph into a vision, giving birth to a figure of light. Was it a man? Perhaps it was, far in the distance, a man glowing with a yellow flame, so bright that he looked like a lighthouse on a dark night at sea. He was singing this song, these words, over and over. I was moving closer to him, moving at tremendous speeds, and as I did, his song grew louder and sharper. It was a different language, but I understood it now.

"*Sound bender, sound bender, sound bender,*" he sang. I knew then, without question, that he was calling my real name. I was Sound Bender.

As I moved closer I began to recognize him. He was familiar, like a recurring character from my dreams. I was almost face-to-face with him. His song filled every crevice of my mind. He wasn't moving his lips — if those were lips — but I heard his voice.

"*You are not alone,*" he told me. "*No one is alone. You are connected to all people, all life, all things through the music of their souls.*"

I gathered my galloping thoughts and rolled them into one question.

"Who are you?" I asked without speaking.

"*I am you. I am me. I am. And I have always been with you. Remember me, and understand that now we know each other. Try to remember, Sound Bender.*"

"I do remember," I told him.

"Now open your secret ears to the music of the universe. To the sound that spans time."

After that, I felt myself drifting off, like I was falling asleep. Just the ocean waves crashing and returning to the deep sea. I felt as if I were returning with those waves, and the farther out to sea I floated, the less I was aware. Until everything was just darkness.

CHAPTER 9

When I woke up, the world was blurry. My head was killing me and my temples were throbbing. I felt like I was wearing a really thick pair of glasses. In fact, every part of my body hurt. That song, that strange familiar song, was playing in my head, but I couldn't hear all of it. I tried to scream out, but the only sound I could muster was a pathetic moan. My mouth and throat were so dry that I sounded like a dying man in the desert.

"Here, drink some water," someone said.

I felt a cool glass on my lips and water in my mouth. I'd never tasted anything so good. As my helper poured another sip in my mouth, my eyesight began to sharpen, and as it did, the song in my head began to fade into the distance.

"He's awake!" I heard my helper shout.

I tried to speak, but again, all that came out was a groan. I blinked my eyes hard several times — I could see glowing afterimages. Afterimages of what? Something bright and shiny, like fireflies, but I didn't know what.

Slowly I began to realize that I was in my spaceship bed at Crane's penthouse, but I couldn't remember how I'd gotten there. The last thing I remembered was walking to Jeremy's record store with Trevor. Then a big fat blank. It was like trying to remember a dream hours after you've woken up. You know it's there, but it's hazy and slipping away.

Another sip of water and my sight started to return to normal. I saw hands near my face — small hands. I followed the arms up to a face.

"Dmitri?" I whispered hoarsely.

"Hello, Leo," he said. "He's up," he shouted again.

"What are . . . where am . . . "

"Shh. Rest, Leo."

"Well, good morning, Master Rip Van Winkle. Or should I say good afternoon?" It was Crane. I couldn't see him well — he was just a blob — but I'd know that lizardy voice anywhere.

"Hollis, come see your sleepy brother," he called out. "And bring his gangly friend as well."

I scooched up in bed to get a better view. My sight was coming back. I was in my room in Crane's penthouse apartment. He was standing in the doorway, looking uncomfortable and afraid to enter. I saw Hollis and Trevor squeeze by him and come over to me. Hollis looked terrified —

his eyes were all squinty and his forehead filled with worry lines.

"Leo?" he said. His voice sounded nervous. Of course he was. I know how I'd feel if something bad happened to him. We're all we have.

"I'm okay, chief," I said. "What happened?"

Actually, I was feeling somewhat better. My vision was clear and my head wasn't throbbing nearly as much.

"I'll have Olga heat up some soup, Leo," Crane said from the doorway. "Dmitri will bring it in when it's ready. Come, Dmitri."

"But I want to stay with the guys," Dmitri said.

Crane sighed and made a clicking sound, and with that, Dmitri bounced up from my bed and trotted after Crane as he left my room.

"You all right, man?" Trevor asked me once the door shut. "We were worried about you."

"Yeah," Hollis echoed, pacing back and forth. "What's with you?"

"I think I'm okay now. But this bed is killing me. What time is it?" I asked.

Hollis slid open his phone. I noticed it was a brand-new one.

"Where'd you get that?" I asked him.

"A present from Uncle Crane. It's 4:37 p.m. You've been asleep for almost twenty-two hours."

"You're kidding," I said. From this windowless room, it was impossible to tell what time it was.

"I thought we should've taken you to the hospital," Trevor explained, "but Jeremy insisted we bring you here and let your uncle Crane decide."

"He wasn't here when they brought you in," Hollis said, "so I called him. Man, was he pissed. He was at dinner with an Italian guy, trying to buy some painting of Jesus as a baby. He said he blew the deal because he had to leave to take care of you. You're probably grounded for life."

"I don't remember being brought here."

"Your uncle called his doctor who came and checked you out," Trevor said. "He said he didn't see anything wrong, but if it happens again, he's going to run some tests."

"Guys, wait a second," I cut in. "What exactly did happen to me?"

"You seriously don't know?" Trevor asked. "What's the last thing you remember, Leo?"

"Um. Walking to Jeremy's store with you."

Hollis stopped pacing and was now busy flicking this little piece of paper around on my desk.

"Do you remember why we were going to his store?" Trevor asked.

I thought about it hard, but every time I tried to remember, that strange half melody would pop back into my head. It was the same one from the other day, when I first got the blue disc. That's right, the blue disc! It was coming back to me now.

"We were going to find out more about that disc from my d—" I cut myself off and looked at Hollis. He stopped flicking the paper around. He knew that I was keeping something from him, something "adult."

"Hollis, could you give me and Trevor a second?"

He flicked the paper hard, and it flew off the table and popped against the wall, right next to my head.

"Fine," he snapped, acting just like the child that I was treating him as. "I'll go watch TV and you and Trevor can discuss your mental illness." He stomped out of my room, slammed my door, slammed his door, and then turned on his TV at an incredible volume.

"Did you tell him about the disc?" I asked Trevor.

"No, I didn't, Leo. But I think you should tell him. He has a right to know."

"I will, Trev. But I have to figure out a few things first. Like what happened to me."

"Okay. We went to Jeremy's store and you showed him that blue disc that you said was from your dad. And then we went to Stinky Steve's crazy apartment for you to listen to it."

"The zombie plate lady . . . " It was all coming back.

"You got it. You asked to be left alone to hear it, so I watched *Jeopardy!* with him and the old lady, who by the way, totally pummeled me. When you didn't come out after *Final Jeopardy!* we went in. You were passed out on the floor with your mouth open. Cold as ice, but covered in sweat. You were drifting in and out, and speaking in a strange language. I called Jeremy, and he and I loaded you in a cab and brought you to your uncle's. And thank you very much, you drooled all over my favorite sweatshirt."

"It's all pretty hazy," I said.

"You're probably still in shock. Klevko and that son of his got you into bed, and I went home. That was yesterday. Today is Tuesday, and I came here after school to see how you're doing. That's the whole story, except you might want to know that Abby Two asked where you were in Spanish class."

Abby Two. Beautiful Abby Two. Suddenly, I remembered hearing her dad's voice when I touched her pen. The memory made me shudder involuntarily. Trevor leaned down to me and looked me dead in the eye.

"Leezer, there's something you're not telling me. Are you sick with some kind of bad disease?"

"No, I'm not sick."

"So what is it then? The grief pamphlet didn't mention anything about passing out for no reason."

"I have been experiencing some things, but . . . you'll think I'm crazy if I tell you."

"I already think you're crazy, and I'm cool with that. Leo, listen to me. I'm your friend, maybe I can help with whatever it is."

"Okay, there is something going on, Trev. It started with that disc from my dad and this letter I received from him. He told me to keep it all a secret. Do you promise never to tell?"

"I swear," he said. "On the grave of Sir Isaac Newton."

"I'm serious, Trev."

"So was Isaac Newton."

I took a breath to begin the story, but before I got the first word out, the door opened and Dmitri came in carrying a fancy silver tray with a bowl of steaming soup. I suddenly realized that I was starving.

"That soup smells great, Dmitri! Can you put it over there on the desk?"

"No, I'll help you drink it, like before."

"Thanks, buddy, but I'll help him," Trevor said. "We're sort of talking man stuff here."

Dmitri pouted. "I'll wait outside. Crane wants to make sure that Leo drinks all of his soup. My *matka* made it from scratch. It will make you strong like me."

He put the tray down on the desk and left. I was still a little wobbly, but Trevor helped me get out of bed and walk over to the desk.

"Put a little food in your belly, then you'll tell me everything," he said.

The soup looked delicious. I wondered if I could get Dmitri to ask his *matka* to make me a grilled cheese sandwich, too. That's what my mom always made for me whenever I got sick, and it was so good that I was almost glad to get the flu.

As soon as I picked up the spoon, I knew something was wrong. It felt weird in my hand, electric almost. The hairs on the back of my neck stood on end, and when I looked at the spoon, it seemed almost transparent, swirling with that bright light. *Oh no. It was happening again.* The sound of the ocean rose in my ears. Lights streaked across my vision until they got so bright and pulsating that they faded away. Then I was alone in the darkness, listening to the tide. I remembered this place. And I heard that song. It was everywhere, not loud, but all around me, inside me — maybe it was me.

I heard something new. Voices. I recognized those voices. It was Klevko and Olga, and they were talking. The light swirled in time to their voices, yet they sounded like they were right next to me.

"No, no, no, Olga. I told you no chicken feet in the soup."

"He will not know."

"Yes, he will know. American boys have weak stomachs."

"Chicken feet give the soup flavor. It will make him strong, like Dmitri."

"It will make him sick. He needs American soup."

"What's the matter, Klevko? Are you ashamed of Polish soup? My mother put chicken feet in her soup, her mother use chicken feet—"

"Fine, Olga. I will take feet out myself."

Then I heard a struggle, followed by two loud smacks.

"You hit me with the soup spoon, Olga, you mean woman."

"I am mean like your mother, because you don't listen. I smack you again every time you try to touch my soup."

"You are so mean, Olga. You are the only woman I love."

Then it was quiet and the swirling lights faded away. Slowly, I came out of the darkness and the light returned, dim and shadowy. The sound of the waves grew soft, like ripples in a calm lake. In that twilight instant, I remembered everything that had happened the day before — the sounds on the blue disc, the rhythmic drumming, the haunting melody, and the radiant figure who emerged from the light. I felt completely happy. Nothing hurt. I was light as air. I didn't even feel sad about my parents. It was as if they were there with me, watching me — as if they weren't even dead. They were still alive in my mind. And that was okay. Everything was okay.

Please let me remember this. Please let me remember this feeling when I wake up.

Suddenly, I felt a snap and a voice calling me.

"Hey! Leezer! Where are you, man?"

I jerked back into reality, like you do when you catch yourself falling asleep in class. I was holding the spoon in my hand but dropped it instantly and it fell with a clatter onto the tray. It was a normal spoon.

"You zoned out there, Leo," Trevor said, looking at me curiously. "For like five seconds or so."

"Trev, could you get Dmitri?"

"What do you want with *him*?"

"Just get him. I'll explain later."

Trevor squinted at me, shrugged, then went and rounded up Dmitri, who was lurking out in the hall, just like he said he would.

"It's good soup, eh?" he said, strutting back in like a returning hero.

"Dmitri, does your mom use chicken feet in her soup?"

He took a step back and scrunched up his face.

"Don't worry," I said. "I'm not insulting your mom's soup. I just want to know. Does she use chicken feet in her soup?"

"This is not for me to discuss." Dmitri walked directly over to my bed, sat down on the pillow, and pushed the number 34 on the control panel.

"Not the pillow again, dude," I said, mostly to myself.

Literally ten seconds later, Klevko trotted into the room wearing a big grin on his face.

"Hullo, Leo! I'm so happy to see you. Sometimes you have to sleep like an animal to feel like a man, yes?"

Klevko was so genuinely glad to see me that I felt bad for what I was about to do. But I had to show Trevor, so that when I told him the strange truth—that I heard Klevko's and Olga's voices when I touched the spoon—he'd believe me.

"Klevko, Dmitri has something to ask you," I said.

Dmitri lowered his head. "Leo wants to know, does Matka use chicken feet in her soup?"

Klevko looked like he had seen a ghost. He slunk down and I swear I saw all the blood rush out of his face.

"No," he said. "Never chicken feet. It's disgusting." And then he faked spitting onto the floor and grimaced.

"Klevko," I said. "I know she does."

I was so cool, so confident in my claim. I could see that I had him. He looked like a little kid who was caught stealing. It was almost painful to watch.

"Yes, it's true!" he cried. "I tell Olga, no, no, American boys do not eat chicken feet. But she's as mean as my *matka*. She hit me several times with the spoon. She doesn't listen. Don't tell Crane about the chicken feet, please, Leo. He'll fire me for sure."

"Oh no, Klevko. Don't worry. My own mom used chicken feet, too. I love them. Tell Olga, I love her soup. It's all okay, man."

While I was talking, it was like watching Klevko in reverse. All the blood ran back to his face, he stood up straighter, and he was beaming from ear to ear. Then he flexed his muscles.

"Okay, Leo. I'll tell her. Come on, Dmitri, let's surprise Matka with the good news that Leo is feeling much better."

After they left, Trevor sat down at the foot of my bed and shook his head at me. I leaned back confidently in my chair.

"Truth time. Your mom didn't put chicken feet in her soup, did she?"

"Nope."

"So you want to tell me about this? And you can start with where you were when you zoned out a second ago."

Trevor had figured out a lot. I could see his brilliant mind putting all the parts of the puzzle together. The pen at school. The blue disc. The spoon. My mysterious illness. He knew they were all connected.

But even a mind as brilliant as Trevor's would not have guessed the truth of what I already knew — that I could hear the past.

CHAPTER 10

You're full of it," he said at last.

I had told Trevor everything. I didn't leave out a thing, not the islanders, not the shaman in yellow, not the voice who named me Sound Bender. As I spoke, I realized how far out it sounded. I was relieved that Trevor listened without saying a word and seemed to take it all in. When I was finished, he got up, paced around my bedroom, thinking. *You're full of it*, his words kept echoing in my ears. That was not what I wanted to hear. It felt like judgment. To be honest, I was tremendously disappointed in him. I wanted him to believe me, to trust that I was telling the truth.

"The reason I told you all this, Trev, was because you said you were open to believe anything. Remember yesterday, when we were talking about my psychic brain? You said it yourself. 'I'm open to anything.'"

"I am open to it—providing there is evidence, Leo. Evidence is what separates science from hogwash."

"So what now? You think I'm crazy?"

He pulled a little spiral notebook from his jacket. Trevor is never without his spiral notebook and mechanical pencil. He looked around for somewhere to perch, and, when he couldn't find any place, leaned against the wall and jotted down some notes.

"The way I see it," he said when he had finished writing, "there are three possible hypotheses for what's going on with you. The first is you're crazy." I grimaced when he said that. "Face it, Leo. You're saying you have a secret ear that hears spoons and pens talking. That's not exactly normal."

"Can we move on to theory two?" I asked.

"Sure. Number two. It's possible that you're suffering from some kind of post-traumatic stress syndrome because of the plane . . . you know . . . what happened to your parents. Grief can make your mind play weird tricks on you."

I had to acknowledge that theory made a lot of sense. Nevertheless, it wasn't ringing true to me. I saw what I saw and heard what I heard. I was sure of that.

"And the third theory is?" I could hear the impatience in my own voice.

"That what you're saying is completely true. But I'd need evidence to buy it. There just isn't anything in science that explains the phenomenon you're describing."

I sighed deeply. I knew I shouldn't be offended that Trevor didn't believe me—that's just his way. He only trusts what you can see, what you can touch, what you can measure and record in a notebook. But I felt sad. There was a distance between Trevor and me that hadn't existed before. The holy man had said that we were all connected. But I felt very alone, with a huge valley of disbelief between me and my best friend. I wondered if my friendship with Trevor would ever be the same. I wished none of this had happened to me. If this terrible lonely feeling was what it meant to be Sound Bender, then I wanted none of it.

Trevor was tapping his pencil nervously on his notebook. "You're angry," he said.

"Frustrated is more like it. I'm not asking you to flush your brain down the toilet, Trev. I just want you with me on this."

"Okay, then," Trevor said. "Let's do some science. Repeat the experiment and see if we get the same results. You said that you were able to hear voices in the spoon just by touching it, right? So the simplest thing to do is to touch something else and see if you get the same result."

"Okay, what should I touch?"

"I guess anything."

Might as well try the wall, I thought. I concentrated hard and touched the wall, expecting to feel an electric suction or something. But I felt nothing, just me touching the wall. I tried another tactic, putting my mind in a super-calm state, like a kung fu master. I guess I was making a pretty ridiculous face because Trevor busted out laughing.

"Hey, what's the big idea?" I snapped.

"It's Bruce Leo, the lost master who talks to walls." Trevor and I had watched about a thousand kung fu DVDs. My old corner store, Yaffa's, sold them for a dollar a piece. I especially liked the ones about the Shaolin monks.

"All right," I said, pulling my hands away from the wall and jamming them into my pockets. "If you're so wise, suggest something else I can touch."

"Are you kidding? Your uncle has rooms and rooms of crazy stuff—go touch some of that. One of those swords maybe?"

"We're not supposed to touch any of Crane's stuff—I mean, *artifacts*. I think I should wait at least a week until I start breaking his rules. That's the orphan code."

"Come on, Leezer. It's all in the name of science."

There was a bounce in Trevor's step as we left my room. I think he was excited about breaking some rules. It's not something he does.

Hollis's door was open, and though I was kind of jogging after Trevor, I snuck a peek in. Hollis was putting together his drum set. He likes to drum when he's mad.

"Want to hang out later?" I said, in an attempt to soothe his ruffled feathers. He didn't answer, just stared at me with animal eyes. Yeah, he was pissed. That stare can melt hardened criminals. I left and followed Trevor into the mask room.

"What do you want to try first?" Trevor asked as I caught up to him.

"Keep your voice down," I whispered. "We have to be quiet so Crane doesn't catch us."

We tiptoed around the room, checking out all the totem poles and African masks and the giant canoe that hung from the ceiling. I looked out of the floor-to-ceiling windows onto the depressing waterfront. It was raining—I had no idea it was raining. I felt like I had been inside this apartment forever.

"What about this ridiculous thing?" Trevor said.

He was standing in front of a mask made out of dark, gnarly wood with frightening red hair that I was sure was real human hair. Even more frightening was its mouth. It was wide open and inside you could see another head, smaller and looking out. Either the guy in the mask had eaten the baby or he was regurgitating it.

"I'll try it," I said. "Maybe we'll find out why he ate his friend." Trevor reached for his spiral notebook.

I made my eyes all unfocused, like when you're looking at those 3-D posters, and took a slow, relaxing breath. I reached my hand out and touched the red hair. Nothing. I moved my hand over to the baby in its mouth. Still nothing. Out of the corner of my eye, I saw Trevor staring at me like I was a lab rat. He thought I was in a trance.

"I'm going to eat you, Trevor," I growled. He jumped back, dropped his notebook, and almost collided into the floating canoe. I cracked up.

"You idiot, Leo. Be serious."

"Hey, did you hear that?" I asked. "Sounded like footsteps."

We just stood there for a minute, two guilty criminals somewhere between fight and flight. The footsteps pattered down the hall coming closer and closer to us, paused, then scampered away.

"Why do I think it's your nosy pal Dmitri?" Trevor said.

"The kid does seem to pop up out of nowhere. I think he likes us."

"I think he should mind his own business. What about the mask, anything at all?"

"Nada."

"That's okay. This is good. Now we know that it doesn't work on everything." He scribbled more notes.

I let go of the mask and searched the room for my next target.

"How about the canoe?" I suggested. "Maybe the bigger the object, the louder it talks."

"Okay," Trevor said, "but this time, concentrate."

"I was concentrating last time—"

"No, what I mean is, try to put yourself in the same frame of mind as when you touched the spoon. Maybe your mental state has something to do with it."

Same frame of mind, I thought as I walked to the canoe. I could see out the window. Man, it was a gray day. Ice-cold rain. What was I thinking when I touched the spoon? I remember trying to get that faraway song out of my head so I could eat my soup in peace. *The song! Could that be it?* I tried to focus all my thoughts on the song as I reached out and touched the painted wood of the canoe.

Nothing.

Trevor had circled around and was observing me with his scientist look again. I moved my hand to another spot on the canoe. Still nothing. I shook my head at Trevor.

"Were you concentrating like we discussed?" he asked.

"Yup."

"Why don't you touch some of the totem poles? That one of the bird with the yellow feathers looks interesting. Try that one. But just relax, don't force it."

I touched the bird totem pole and waited. Nothing happened. I felt like crying. Why wasn't this working? Because I was crazy, that's why. Because I had imagined the whole thing. In a fit, I ran to the next totem pole and touched it. Nothing. Then the next one. Nothing. I ran all over the room, brushing my hand against every object I could touch.

Nothing. Nothing. And more nothing.

"This has to work!" I shouted as I chased my shadow around the room. I was losing control, and I knew it. I froze when I heard a beeping. It was Trevor's phone. He pulled it from his pocket, read a text, then looked at me like he had bad news.

"Hey, Leo, I have to go. I'm sorry, man. I have plans to fix this old radio with my dad tonight." I saw him wince. I knew he was thinking that just talking about his living dad would make me feel bad. It didn't, though. "I'll call you tonight after I'm done, and we'll figure this out, okay?"

I was so frustrated and upset that I couldn't even bring myself to answer. I wandered over to the window and looked out at the river below. I was sure Trevor was secretly laughing at me. Who wouldn't? Even that old man in the photo was laughing at me. I picked up a framed photograph that was sitting on the window ledge. Inside was a yellowed picture of a guy in uniform, resting his foot on a tank, grinning out at me.

"That's right, I'm a nutcase," I said to the photo. "I just have to accept it, I guess."

I thought I saw a flash of lightning shooting across the window, but it wasn't lightning. It was my vision, starting to pulse. Then, from out of nowhere, shots rang out . . . machine guns firing in the distance. The sound of airplane propellers surrounded me. It sounded like fighter-bombers from those old black-and-white war movies.

"Stay down in the trenches, men!" I heard a voice call. "The Germans are advancing on us!"

The sound of more gunshots rang in my head, artillery of all kinds. A barrage of shells whizzed by my ears and I ducked for cover.

"I'm caught on the barbed wire, Captain. You have to move on!" The voice sounded terrified, and the panic in his voice flooded my body.

"Hold on, Al. I'm coming for you," the captain's voice responded.

"No time. He's got a grenade! Captain . . . watch out!"

There was a loud explosion and a man shrieked in pain — my whole body felt his agony. Then all was silent.

"Leo! Leo! Talk to me, man."

I opened my eyes, and Trevor was standing in front of me, pulling the framed photograph out of my hands.

"What happened?" I asked.

"I was on my way out, and suddenly, you started screaming . . . something about the Germans in the trenches. And barbed wire. Then you doubled over, like you'd been hit in the gut. Where were you, man?"

I looked down at the photograph he was holding, at the man in front of the tank staring out at me.

"I think I was there," I said. "With him."

Trevor reached for his notebook and started to write furiously. "Whoa," he whispered. "This could be a break-through. Tell me more."

Before I could answer, the sound of footsteps appeared, expensive leather shoes squeaking toward us. It was Crane, no doubt about it.

"What's all this commotion?" he asked, entering the room with his usual stern look. "I thought I told you young-sters my possessions were off-limits to you."

"Leo was just walking me to the elevator, sir," Trevor stam-mered. "And we stopped here to admire your excellent view."

Crane glanced suspiciously over at me. I was still stand-ing by the window, the framed photograph of the soldier on the ledge by my side.

"Well, Leo, I see you've found your namesake," he said.

"Huh?"

"If you haven't heard something I've said, Leo, you say 'I beg your pardon, Uncle Crane,' not 'huh.' That sounds like some kind of unpleasant animal noise."

"I beg your pardon, Uncle Crane."

He strode over to me and took the photo into his hands. "This is your great-grandfather. You were named after him. He was a captain in World War I, killed during the Second Battle of Somme on the Western Front. They say he was something of a hero . . . died trying to rescue one of his men who was trapped in the trenches by German barbed wire. A grenade took him down, I believe."

I looked at Trevor and he looked at me. Neither one of us could hide our astonishment. Crane was puzzled by the shock on our faces.

"I hope your family history doesn't shock you, Leo," he said. "I was certain your father would have told you all about it."

I was shocked all right, and so was Trevor. But it had nothing to do with my family history and everything to do with what I had just experienced. The planes, the voices, the gunshots, the explosion. I had heard them all.

"Maybe you really are Sound Bender," Trevor whispered to me and I nodded. "Maybe," he added.

This was big. And we both knew it.

CHAPTER 11

Uncle Crane was leaving for a cocktail party at the Museum of Natural History, and he insisted on dropping Trevor off at home. I wanted him to stay so we could run some more experiments, but Crane was firm.

"You must complete your homework and get to bed early, Leo," he told me. "Tomorrow is a school day and you've been ill. You need to bounce back. Discipline and resilience, those are the keys to success."

Trevor was pretty excited about riding home in the limo, so he didn't put up much argument. We agreed to meet before school in the library, so we could talk.

I felt bad that Hollis was still sulking in his room, so I went down the hall to find him and apologize. I decided not to tell him about my sound-bending power. I would tell him when I understood more, when I was sure that it was real, when I was sure I was safe.

I pushed the door to his room open. His drums were all set up, like they had always been there.

"Wow, you put those together fast," I said.

"Dmitri helped," he said, not even looking up.

"Oh, so you two are friends now?"

"What's it to you, Leo?" This time he did look up, and gave me a stare that was somewhere between angry and hurt. Correct that. It was just flat-out angry. He turned his back to me and opened a big cardboard box. Inside was his Wurlitzer 200A keyboard and stand. Crane's men had delivered all our things that afternoon. Hollis had way more boxes than I did. He had a lot of instruments, clothes, sports equipment. I tended to wear the same thing most days and my sound equipment, although very advanced, could all fit into one box.

"Feel like exploring?" I said. "Crane's gone and we have the place to ourselves."

"You've been kind of a jerk, bro, in case you hadn't noticed."

"I'm sorry, Hollis. Come on, let's hang out."

"I've got to set up my Wurlitzer," he said.

"You can do that later, and you know it. Come on. I'm asking you nicely."

Even though he was mad, I could see Hollis weakening. There must have been a part of him that was relieved to get the invitation. We've had our share of fights, that's for sure, but in the end, one of us always gives in, usually me.

We wandered down the hall and into the main rooms, past the totem poles and over the glass bridge into the sword room. The sun had set and everything in there had a shadowy look except for the silver reflections shimmering off the blades of the swords.

"I wonder where Crane sleeps," Hollis said. "There's no beds anywhere here."

"I will show you, if you want." The voice seemed to be coming from the suit of armor in the middle of the room.

Hollis jumped sky high. "Did you say something, dude?" he said to the suit of armor.

Dmitri popped out from behind the armor and flashed us his crooked little smile. It was weird how he always seemed to know where we were. It was like he was following us, always lurking. I don't like lurkers.

"How'd you get here?" I asked him.

"This building is my place," he said. "I know every corner. Crane has many rooms, secret rooms. I'm not supposed to tell anyone, but since Hollis and I are best friends, I will show you."

I glanced over at Hollis.

"Best friends?" I whispered.

"According to him," he whispered back.

By then, Dmitri had walked across the room and was standing right next to us. I had noticed that both he and Klevko had a very close sense of personal distance. Like unless they could breathe on you, they weren't close enough. That made me extremely uncomfortable.

"We can see the place some other time, Dmitri," I said, taking a few steps back. The truth was I didn't want to owe this kid a favor. There was something untrustworthy about him. Why was he always skulking around after us in the shadows?

"Secret rooms?" Hollis said. "I want to see them for sure."

I could tell that he and Dmitri actually were becoming friends and made a mental note to talk to him about that.

Dmitri grabbed the left pinkie of the suit of armor and twisted it. I heard a faint sliding sound. Really? A secret passage? Oh, that was so like Crane. You could feel that he was a man of many secrets. I looked around in the dim light, and found what I assumed was the doorway, not a grand entrance but just a slender slit in between the flat-screen TV and the window. It was so small — I could hardly imagine Crane fitting in there.

We followed Dmitri into the tiny passage that led down a long hall. At the end of the hall was a single black door with a brass knob. Dmitri pushed a button on the wall, and the secret doorway slid shut behind us as the black door in front of us swung open. Inside was a tiny elevator just big enough for one full-size adult. The three of us jammed in. I noticed that the elevator had only two buttons: Cloud Room and D.N.D. Room.

"I will show you the Cloud Room," Dmitri said, pushing the button.

"What's the D.N.D. Room?" I asked.

"It stands for Do Not Disturb. No one but Crane is allowed there. I snuck inside once."

"Wow. What was in there?" Hollis asked.

"A safe so big, it took up almost half the room," Dmitri answered in a secretive tone. "And rifles on the wall. Many rifles."

"Does Crane hunt?" I asked.

"No."

"Then why does he have all those rifles?"

"Why does anyone have rifles?" Dmitri said. "To shoot things."

"Did you see inside the safe?" Hollis asked. "I bet it was full of money."

"And gold and silver."

"Cool," Hollis said. "Like pirate treasure."

Ever since our parents took us to Disney World, Hollis has been obsessed with the Pirates of the Caribbean ride, so the idea of pirate treasure was right up his alley. His eyes were practically popping out of his head.

The elevator stopped with a jerk. When we got out, I had the feeling that we hadn't gone up but had traveled sideways, to a place inside the building. We were in a waiting room, with a large receptionist's desk but no receptionist. I felt like I was in a spy movie, in one of those secret interrogation rooms.

"Why does he call this the Cloud Room?" I asked.

"Go in and you will see."

We went in and even though the room was dark, moonlight flooded in from the ceiling. There were tables with objects scattered around the room, but the thing that caught my eye was that the entire ceiling was made of glass. It arched into a sphere in the center, like an observatory dome. On a platform in the middle of the dome stood a large telescope.

"I didn't know Crane liked astronomy," I said.

"He doesn't," Dmitri answered. Again, that crooked smile.

"Then what's the point of this humungous telescope?" Hollis asked.

"There are many things to look at beside stars," Dmitri answered.

I climbed the steps to the platform and looked through the telescope. Oddly, it wasn't pointed at the sky, but at the city around us and the river below. I swiveled it to the left and saw Finkelstein's salami factory in much more detail than I would have liked. Through the windows, I could make out men in bloody aprons grinding meat in large stainless steel containers. Quickly, I moved the lens to the right and saw the East River and the wharf that extended from Crane's warehouse. When I focused in, I saw a boat tied up to Crane's wharf. I couldn't see much, but it had a small hold for cargo and a Chinese dragon painted on its side. A uniformed guard was pacing back and forth in front of it.

Hollis was blown away by the whole scene. He would have stayed there the entire night, touching each object on the polished tables around the room. An amethyst geode the size of a human head. An etched Viking shield. A carved ivory pipe in the shape of a frog. A complete set of zebra hooves. But Dmitri was starting to get nervous. It's a good thing we left when we did, because no sooner had we slid out through the narrow secret passage and returned to the sword room than Klevko appeared.

"Boys! I came to look for you. Crane, he called to say you must stay in your rooms and do homework. Olga will bring you dinner there."

"Can I hang out with the guys?" Dmitri asked. "Please, Oji."

"No, son. You have promised your mother to play canasta with her tonight." Turning to us, he explained. "Canasta is a card game we play in Poland. We play sneaky like foxes. You must join us sometime."

"Sounds like a blast," Hollis said. Klevko threw his head back and slapped his belly.

Hollis and I went back to our rooms. While he did his homework and practiced his drums, I surfed the net, reading about small islands off the coast of Papua New Guinea. Aua. Manu. Wuvulu. Takuu. Tuvalu. Even the names sounded soft and welcoming. Was one of them my birthplace? I had so many questions, and not one answer.

Later, I hung out in Hollis's room and we watched some TV. I noticed that he had set up a little bookshelf on his desk. It definitely gave the starkness of his room a homier feel. Before long, he fell asleep. I flicked off the TV and, on my way out, stopped and looked at his books. One copy of *Yachting* magazine, the Guinness Book of

World Records, *Understanding the Stock Market for Kids*, and *The Runaway Bunny*. It was a book our mom read to us every night.

I picked up the book, went to my room, and flopped down on my bed. I rolled over on my side and opened the book. I almost didn't need to — I knew it all by heart. I started to read the first page.

"Once there was a little bunny who wanted to run away. So he said to his mother, 'I am running away.'"

Without warning, the voice in my head changed, and suddenly, it wasn't me reading, but my mother, her voice so soothing and familiar. The room grew dim and I heard those familiar ocean waves, but I wasn't dizzy or blinded by flashes of light. In fact, I was barely aware of my surroundings at all, just my mother's voice, reading me the story.

"'If you run away,' said his mother. 'I will run after you. For you are my little bunny.'"

My mother's voice paused, and I heard the turn of a page, then the voice of a child perhaps two or three years old.

"Mommy, can I have some apple juice in a bottle?" it said.

"No, Leo," came my mom's voice, clearly now. "You're a big boy. Even your little brother, Hollis, doesn't drink from a bottle anymore."

"But I don't want to be a big boy. I just want my bottle!"

The little kid began to cry and I realized it was me. It was as if I was two years old, and I was hearing myself, feeling my sad little boy self.

Instinctively, I let go of the book and within seconds, the boy's cry disappeared. I blinked, looked around, and saw that I was there, in my spaceship room in my uncle's apartment.

CHAPTER 12

revor," I said, running up to him in the library the next morning. "I have a new theory. Listen to this. What I realized was —"

"Ease up, Leo. A little privacy would be good here."

We were standing in the middle of the library, and I realized there were a bunch of kids around, not to mention Ms. Pontoon, the librarian. Trevor took my arm and led me over to a couple of chairs in the computer area.

"You don't want to be sharing this stuff with the world quite yet," he warned. "There still is the crazy factor, you know."

"Good point, Trev."

I pulled the orange plastic chair up next to him, sat down, and lowered my voice. "So last night, you're not going to believe this, but —"

I heard someone laughing. Two girls — I think it was Lisa Murphy and Maya Amine — had gotten up from the table where they were sitting, and moved closer to us. When they caught my eye, they burst into uncontrollable giggles and one of them waved. I checked my fly to make sure it wasn't open. I couldn't imagine any other reason why they'd be giggling at me. I wasn't the kind of guy cute girls giggled at.

"What's that about?" I whispered to Trevor.

"Everyone's talking about you today, Leezer. When you and Hollis pulled up to school in the limo . . . you're legendary now. People want to know more."

"Like why we're rich and stuff? Hollis can tell them," I said. "He loves that."

I have to confess, I did notice that a lot of people said hi to me in the hall on my way to the library. People like Justin Winters and his soccer team pals, who didn't usually give me much attention. Okay, any attention. I'm not saying it made my day or anything, to have those guys saying hi to me or Lisa and Maya flirting with me. But I will say this — being included is not the worst feeling in the world.

"So what's this brilliant new theory?" Trevor whispered. I gave Maya a cool little wave, which was probably not nearly as cool as I thought it was, then turned to Trev. I spoke in a hushed tone.

"I think I have to be drawn to the thing," I said.

He shook his head. "We're talking science here, bud. Throw me a word, a concept, a theory, anything the left side of the human brain can latch on to."

I nodded. It was so clear to me that I'd probably skipped a couple steps in my explanation.

"Okay, here it is. When I touch some objects, I hear nothing, right? But there are others that I have a connection to—and when I touch them, I can hear the past. Sound bend. They talk to me, Trev."

"We'll have to experiment more with that idea," Trevor said, rubbing his chin, which I noticed was sprouting some minor peach fuzz.

"I did. I practiced half the night. A book from my childhood, my ten-speed bike, Hollis's stuffed elephant—it worked with all of them. And the more I practiced, the easier it got. Fewer blinking lights and dizzy spells, too—just me and the sound. I'm getting better and better at this."

"I'm going to have to see it to believe it, Leo."

"Fine, I'll demonstrate," I said, full of confidence. "Follow me."

We walked over to Maya and Lisa, who were still turning around to catch glances of us. I pretended to trip over Maya's backpack, which was on the floor by her feet. When I bent down to pick it up, I clutched it tight and concentrated.

"Don't forget your backpack!" I heard a mom-type voice call out.

"I can't find it," came the response.

"Use your brother's. The bus will be here any minute."

"But it stinks like gym socks," the girl's voice said.

"Take it, Maya, or you'll miss the bus."

As I handed the backpack to Maya, the voices died down instantly and I was back in the library, almost like nothing had happened.

"Here's your backpack," I said to Maya. "Better give it back to your brother."

She looked surprised. "How'd you know it was his?"

I shrugged. "I sit behind you in Life Science," I said. "Your backpack is red, with a pink and white penguin key chain on the zipper."

"I didn't think you noticed, Leo," she said with a nice smile.

"And tell your brother to change his gym socks more often."

She laughed. As Trevor and I walked off and headed to our homerooms, we discussed what had happened. I was in a good mood, but he was looking worried.

"Don't you think we should tell someone about this power of yours?" he said.

"Like Hollis? Or Jeremy?"

"No, like the CIA or the government or the *Skeptical Inquirer* or somebody. I don't know whom to tell, now that I think of it. What you have, Leo, is something phenomenal. It could change everything we know about how the world works."

"It belongs to me. To us."

"Sure, but Leo, science is based on openness. We have to—"

"We will Trev. My dad said to keep it secret, and he must have had his reasons."

Everywhere I went in school that day, I picked up objects to see what I could hear. Trevor followed me around, taking notes in his spiral notebook. It didn't work all the time, that's for sure. With at least half the items I picked up, I couldn't channel one sound, not a peep. Mr. Judd's roll book, Principal Bauer's reading glasses, Wilson Yee's brown bag lunch were all duds.

But when I *was* able to channel an object, it was a blast. Like finding out that Matthew Boyd was not going to get the lead in the school play. That guy is so full of himself, and for no good reason. When I touched the curtain on the stage in the auditorium where they hold school auditions, I heard the drama teachers telling each other that Matthew Boyd was "not leading man material."

I was able to connect really well with Trevor's science fair poster. It felt great to let him know that his study of the mathematics of snowflakes was going to take first place. Boy, the teachers couldn't have raved more. As I held on to his poster board, the words *fantastic, brilliant, genius* repeated over and over in my head.

We carried my mini recorder around all day and tried to capture what I was hearing. When the voices were just in my head, nothing appeared on the tape recorder, only the sound of my breathing. But when I held a violin in the music room, the sound in my head was really powerful and I sometimes made faint sounds with my mouth and throat.

In Algebra, Mr. Judd asked me to pass back the irrational numbers unit exams. When I came to Madison McAndrews, I stopped at her desk and held her test for an extra second. I couldn't hear much, but when I ran my hand along it, I did hear a single sentence. She was telling her best friend that she studied for six hours. No wonder she won the Math Olympiad.

At lunch, Trevor and I went into the cafeteria. I gave him a tray, and took one for myself, sliding it along the counter until I got to the mac and cheese area.

"I'm going to get another tray," I said, almost immediately after I touched it.

"Is that one wet? I hate the smell of wet plastic," Trevor said.

"It's dry, but it just feels negative."

"A negative cafeteria tray?" Trevor shot me a look. "Get a grip."

I had to admit this did sound crazy. But I swear, touching that tray gave me a bad feeling. As I held it, I suddenly heard a whooshing in my ears, like the sound of a sled careening down an icy hill.

"Woo hoo, man! I'm flying!" a voice in my head rang out.

Then I heard a scraping sound, like something was being dragged over rough concrete. And then the screech of car brakes and a horn blaring.

I opened my eyes and took my hands off the tray. I understood now. In November, just after the first snow, two eighth-grade boys had taken school cafeteria trays outside and used them as sleds. They went to Riverside Park, where they sat on them and went sliding down the hill. One of them, Richard Moffee, went out of control, flew into the street, and was almost hit by a car. A police officer brought them both back to school, and they got suspended for a week.

"I have Richard Moffee's tray," I told Trevor.

"You sure?"

I nodded. "I heard it. The accident."

Someone tapped me on the shoulder.

"Mind if I cut in line?" It was Abby Two. "Maybe we can have lunch together."

"You guys go ahead," Trevor said. "I have to finish my science project display. Last-minute touches. See you after school, Leo."

"Don't forget you're coming back to my house," I called after him.

As Trevor paid for his tuna sandwich and ran off, Abby took a green salad from the line. I grabbed a mac and cheese. Hollis was a couple tables away, surrounded by friends. I could hear him telling everyone the features of Crane's limo.

"That's quite a car you and your brother have these days," Abby said, pouring some ranch dressing onto her salad. "Maybe you can take me for a ride in it sometime."

"I'll ask my uncle," I said. "It's got a lot of cool stuff. Iced Cokes whenever you want one."

There was silence as we started to eat. Man, was I nervous. I couldn't think of anything to say.

"I love ranch dressing," I finally said, when the silence had gotten almost too much to bear. "I could eat it on anything. Chicken, pizza, salad, broccoli. Even cauliflower. You name it."

Abby Two didn't look up. Can you blame her? How pathetic am I? I thought. Like she cares about my ranch dressing fixation. I felt my mouth get dry and my brain start to race. Think of something to say, Leo. She's expecting you to be interesting. Come up with something. And not ranch dressing.

In desperation, I opened my mouth and started to talk.

"I was there when Richard Moffee almost got creamed," I said.

That got her attention.

"Really? Everybody was talking about it for days. Tell me about it."

I took a big bite of mac and cheese to stall, then put both hands on my tray and held on tight. And it spoke to me. I listened and heard every detail. The brakes squealing. The angry driver. The discovery of the tray. The pathetic lie Richard Moffee told. The arrival of the police officer. The return to school. The meeting in Principal Bauer's office. The tears. The apology. All the sounds raced into my head in one powerful surge.

Abby Two was waiting, looking at me curiously.

"You're a very slow chewer," she said.

"I love mac and cheese," I said. "You have to appreciate every bite."

I told her the story of the accident, all the little details everyone wanted to know but Principal Bauer said were none of our business. Abby was fascinated. I was telling her something that no one else in school knew. I was amazed at how clearly I saw the picture of what had happened — maybe not in images, but in sound pictures. It was like I had a movie of the whole thing playing in my ears.

After lunch, Abby Two and I walked to our next class together. I confess. It felt great to be walking next to her, to be a part of the seventh-grade social scene. Then, as we turned to head up the stairs, we came face-to-face with Richard Moffee.

"Hey, Leo," he said. "I'm sorry about your parents, man."

He was a nice guy, Richard Moffee. And I had blabbed his personal business. Stuff I had no right even knowing.

All of a sudden, I didn't feel so great anymore.

CHAPTER 13

Driving back to the penthouse, Hollis and Trevor were giddy. For Hollis, the thrill of limo rides had not worn off, and for Trevor, the thrill had just begun. They were having fun playing with the gadgets, staring out at all the people trying to get a glimpse of us through the dark tinted windows to see if we were anyone famous. I wanted to be happy like they were, but I was pretty blue. I felt alone. My power was growing stronger by the hour and I was gaining more and more control over it. That was exhilarating. It made me stand up straighter and be less afraid. It made me more popular. It gave me a way to impress girls — I could still smell Abby Two's vanilla lotion from when she gave me a hug.

Then why did I feel so sad and alone? I thought about my day at school. What I had done was use my power to find out other people's secrets. And for what? A bit of attention? To make more so-called friends? My power should have been drawing people close to me, but oddly, it was doing the opposite. More people were near, but they weren't close. I was a spy. There must be more important uses for it than meeting girls and ratting out a nice guy like Richard Moffee.

As we crossed over the Brooklyn Bridge, I looked out at the green water that led out to the ocean. There had to be a better way.

When the car rolled up to the penthouse, my thoughts were still back on the bridge. Hollis and Trevor tumbled out of the limo and ran ahead into the lobby. I wasn't moving so fast.

"Hey, kiddo. Leo."

It was Stump.

"Unless you want to drive with me to the airport, exit to your right. Crane has some hotshot Russian clients flying in, and I have to beat the traffic."

"Oh, sorry," I said.

"Buck up champ, you're *all right*," he said. When I didn't answer, he reached into his coat pocket and pulled out a bright red straw, just like the ones he was always chewing on.

"Here," he said, handing me the straw. "Life ain't easy. Trust me, I know." He looked down at his half-eaten-away arm. "I've had bad things happen to me. Then I found the straw. Stick it in your mouth, and when you start thinking life stinks, concentrate on the straw. Things won't seem so bad."

"Thanks, Stump." It was the strangest bit of advice I'd ever received, the perfect end to one of the strangest days I'd ever had.

"Now I got to tear out of here or Crane will have my other arm," he said, and true to his word, he tore out of there. I put the straw carefully in my backpack.

It was another cold day in the run-down salami district, but I almost wanted to go for a swim. I felt skuzzy, and I longed to be clean. Trevor came out of the building lobby.

"You ready to get to work?" he asked. We had decided to do more testing on my power, see how it worked on objects in Crane's warehouse.

"Maybe we could just walk over to the river for a second," I said. "I live right on the water, but I haven't even been down there."

We walked around the front side of Crane's building. We didn't talk. Trevor is a good enough friend that we understand we don't have to make conversation if we don't feel like it. The calm water lapped noiselessly onto the gravel shoreline. I found a seat on an old ledge of crumbling cement that was being torn apart from the inside by weeds and watched the ratty seagulls perched on the decaying pier columns, extending their wings and squawking. In the distance, I saw the endless stream of traffic on the Brooklyn Bridge. I wondered what was keeping that giant bridge from collapsing into the water. "London Bridge is falling down, falling down, falling down," kept playing far away in my mind. That song used to terrify me.

Trevor picked up some rocks and started throwing them into the East River. He was trying to skip them, but he had *no arm* — the rocks just landed into the water with a hollow *gulip*. It was strangely soothing. There was something about the water that seemed to pull on me . . . pull me out. The slow tide was churning in my ears. And without being aware of it, that island melody kept drifting in and out of my mind.

I got the red straw out of my backpack and sat there fiddling with it, thinking about Stump. Crane was paying him to drive the limo, but he felt the impulse to reach out to me in his own bizarre way. Maybe he knew that things weren't all bad if you could still do something for someone else. Then it hit me. I didn't have to waste my new power screwing around in school. I could change. All I had to do was change my mind.

Trevor sat down on the ledge next to me.

"Hey, what's that?" he said, motioning to the red straw in my hand.

"Oh, this . . . this is my new magic wand."

"What's it do?" Trevor said.

"Not a thing," I said and chuckled.

"You sound better, Leo. You ready to continue our experiments?"

"In a sec. Let's chuck a few more rocks into the ocean. I'll show you how to get one to skip."

"Really?" Trevor's eyes lit up. Trevor has a lot of pride — he's smart and he knows it. But we both know that he can't throw a ball more than ten feet.

So we spent an hour just chucking rocks into the water like a couple of small-town kids, laughing and joking. When we were both shivering, we went inside the lobby and rang the bell for the elevator. The damp air had attached itself to our faces so that it felt like we were sweating glacier water. My breath was thick as fog. I felt a clammy hand on my shoulder and heard loud mouth breathing.

"In from the cold, boys?" It was Klevko.

"Y-y-y-yeah," Trevor answered, his teeth chattering. He hates the cold. He's so skinny that the air cuts straight to his bones.

"This is nothing," Klevko said. "In Poland, it is cold like for polar bears." Without warning, he growled like a polar bear, right in our faces. And then, I swear, he twitched one of his pec muscles.

Refreshed, Klevko opened the gate into the dilapidated elevator. We bounced our way up and stopped on the fourth floor, then Klevko threw the gate open.

"Hollis and Dmitri are playing on this floor. Go play with them," Klevko said, and gave us a friendly shove.

It was slightly warmer there. Trevor slowly started to straighten out and come out of his turtle shell. He spotted a radiator in the corner, and dashed over there and practically hugged the thing

"Just leave me here, Leo. Go on. Leave. I'm a goner."

"Any last words before I go?"

"Tell 'em I was brave. That I fought till the end. Tell 'em I made it to the summit, and carried an injured man down on my back. That I was a hero."

Trevor took off his parka, gloves, and hat and draped them around the heating vent so they'd be warm when we got back. Always thinking, that Trevor. When he was five, he discovered that if you put some tinfoil on the radiator, you could cook up a pretty decent hot dog in ten to fifteen minutes. When I would sleep over in the winter months, we'd stay up late and eat radiator hot dogs and watch kung fu movies.

We walked through the long aisles of identical crates, looking for something to strike my interest.

"How about this one?" he asked, stopping at a medium-size crate.

I reached out my hand and touched it. "I'm not feeling anything."

We kept walking through aisles and aisles of crates and boxes. Every now and then, Trevor would stop at a random one to see if I wanted to try out the power. I never felt like it, I just wasn't able to connect to anything until—

I stopped.

"Here," I said. "This is the one."

I was by a medium-size crate in Aisle 21, unable to move my feet. There were no identifying marks on the outside of it, no label. Just a long number—11910091005122622—written in black stencil.

As I reached out to touch that crate, a wave of emotion crashed over me. It wasn't any emotion I'd ever felt before. No, this was different. It was directed outward. I felt an incredible sadness for something other than myself, something that was alone and afraid, something that needed my help. In a flash, my mind catapulted back in time to when I was just a toddler, lying alone in my dark room. I was trying to sleep, but I was afraid, awake and terrified of all those strange nighttime sounds in the apartment. A radiator clanking, wood creaking, a lamp making a sound like an owl. How I would dash to my parents' room and tell them, "I heard a sound. Can I stay with you?"

"Any reason for this crate in particular?" Trevor asked, taking out his spiral notebook and mechanical pencil.

I pulled myself back to the present. "No reason," I said. "Just a feeling."

We stood on either side of the crate and braced ourselves to lift it off the others. We were surprised to find it didn't weigh more than ten pounds.

Like all the other crates, this one was nailed shut. Trevor took out his miniature repair kit, and together we worked at prying out the nails. It was slow, boring, and somewhat painful work, but with each nail removed, I felt more and more urgency to get it open. Something was hurting inside there. I had an overriding need to find out more.

We popped the top off. The whole thing was filled with straw. I should have waited, but I couldn't. Plunging my hand into it, I touched a smooth metal object at the bottom of the straw. The minute I made contact with it, I felt the hair rise up on my neck, the tide rise in my ears, and that all-too-familiar feeling of suction. The room had already begun to spin and fade away, and the last thing I saw was Trevor's ghostly image echoing, "What . . . is . . . it . . . Leoooooooooooooo?"

Whatever was in that crate was definitely emitting a powerful force. This was not like the cafeteria tray at school or Maya's backpack or even my great-grandfather's photo. No, from the first touch of the object, I was thrown into a deep, encompassing trance — my mind engulfed in swirling energy and light, followed by complete darkness.

CHAPTER 14

Complete darkness.

I was in the space again, surrounded by unseen tides.

I was calm, at peace. Everything was okay.

In my mind, the distant fireflies flickered faintly. They were everywhere, like twinkling stars on a clear night, and they were crackling like frying bacon. I was streaming toward them, but toward something else, too, something more important. Dozens of whirlpools of light, each a different shade of purple, spun in the darkness and drew me toward them. They wove in and around one another, like a school of darting fish in the ocean. So free and just enjoying the feeling of movement and play.

Their sounds rose in my ears. Low, intense hums at first, followed by what sounded like that sound effect from my old record of a haunted door creaking open and shut. I drew closer to the purple whirlpools. I longed to be a part of them, like watching small kids in the playground and wishing you weren't too old to join in. Three of the purple swirls flashed across my vision, sending out a squeaking noise, like hands running across clean glass. Their sounds and lights surrounded me, until we were all connected by transparent strands of purple light threads.

I felt a part of something. I was one of them. I was a purple swirl. I felt alive — my emotions flowed into one another like waves, from terror to excitement to complete freedom, sharing everything I felt with everyone else instantly and effortlessly. As if we were all a part of music, I was moving like sound. So free. So free.

But then I felt a shadow on the horizon, something dark drawing nearer and nearer to us. A creeping heaviness. Something that would cut the threads between us, and we all knew it. I was overcome by that early childhood fear of the dark as it spread across us, consuming the purple swirls one by one, until there was only a single one left, and it was so little. It stopped moving, then trembled violently until it gave birth to an awful sound, like a cry in the night, so loud that its light exploded in a purple tsunami that crashed over the entire space. I felt the weight of the wave pour into me, fill me to the top, until all I knew was unbelievable sadness and fear. Just like that moment when we found out that our parents were gone, that moment when everything melted away, when no one was there to hold me.

The purple swirl was gone, and all I heard were echoes fading away. But the anguish in that cry still pulsed in my head, the terrible pain and fear. Everything in me wanted to help that purple swirl, but it was too late. Its sadness had spread across the entire space. I felt the energy of my vision slipping away, and the undertow of the real world pulling me into reality.

I snapped back into myself in that familiar way. Trevor had yanked my hand out of the crate, and was looking both concerned and fascinated. Until he spoke, I hardly recognized him.

"Welcome home," he said, handing me a bottle of water he carried in his pocket. "Take a sip. You look like you need it."

I couldn't move. I just sat there holding the bottle in my hand. I felt like I had brought something back with me, like that purple swirl had attached to me. My heart ached with an unknown sadness. I had a burning desire to help. *I needed to help.* But *I* also needed help. That cry was still echoing in my mind, and it made me feel sick. It was so familiar, I couldn't shake the feeling that I had heard it before.

"Am I back on Earth?" I croaked. I was dizzy and light-headed and the colors were still swirling in the corners of my eyes. Our voices sounded booming to me, and the overhead lights were glaring like the sun.

"Yeah, man. Back on planet Earth, well, planet Brooklyn, to be specific."

"Ah, dry land," I said, sort of imitating an old sailor who's spent too many months at sea. I had no idea why I said that.

I wrapped my arms around myself to warm up and rocked back and forth. I mostly wanted to nuzzle into something warm and soft and sleep this away.

"That was a strong connection, huh?" Trevor said. "What'd you hear?"

"It was . . . bacon popping . . . and . . . uh . . . purple spaghetti . . . it's hard to put into words. Can I just relax for a sec?"

"Yeah, sure. Let's check out the crate first and see what caused it."

I hadn't even seen the metal object in the crate. Maybe once I saw it, everything that I experienced would click into place and the lingering, terrible sadness would go away. When Trevor wasn't looking, I wiped the tears out of my eyes and tried to get a hold of myself.

Trevor reached through the straw and pulled out a strange-looking device. His jaw dropped and his mouth froze wide open, dumbfounded.

Whatever it was, it was radiating evil.

It was shaped kind of like a salad bowl, though it definitely wasn't made for salad. The first thing that struck me was the ton of wires that ran along the outside of it. Different colors of wires: red, green, yellow, blue, white, braided together and running over the outside of the bowl shape. The inside of the bowl was made up of strips of black metal that were connected like a jungle gym. Attached to those bars were about a dozen octopus-looking suction cups, like those electrodes people wear when they get brain surgery. Two long straps with a rusted buckle dangled from the sides.

Altogether it was a cruel-looking piece of electronics. I had no idea what it was. Although I was physically beginning to recover from my sound-bending experience, just looking at this thing made my blood boil, as if it were something horrible, like a torture machine.

"I've never seen any electronics like this before," Trevor said.

That was bad news because Trevor could, just by looking, tell almost immediately what any circuit board did.

"It seems to generate power," he went on. "Or transfer power. But there's no power source in it. It must be missing something, because I can't make any sense of this wiring. I think I know this one circuit but . . . " He trailed off and turned the thing around in his hands.

"Hey." He perked up. "I think there's writing in here. Really small and covered by these wires. Let me just push this wire aside."

No sooner had he pushed it than we heard a sharp whoosh, like a switchblade knife being popped open. Trevor startled, and let the thing drop onto the floor. As it wobbled on the cement, both he and I inched closer to it, our heads right next to each other. Two metal needles, one from either side, had shot out from the insides of the bowl toward the center. They were each about four inches long and made of a gray metal.

"Did it get you?" I asked Trevor.

He looked at his hands and turned them over.

"No, I don't think so. What is this—"

"Hey, do you hear that?"

"Yeah," he whispered. We both drew our heads even closer to the thing. It was making small grinding noises, like miniature gears had been activated. Then I saw something that made me sick. From the tips of those needles, two even smaller needles began to emerge, four pointed spikes on each. And as they grew in length, they began to bend, so that they looked like robotic claws, or that piece of dental equipment you pray the dentist never uses on you.

"I don't like this thing," Trevor whispered to me.

"Me neither."

"It feels kind of . . . kind of . . ."

"Evil," I whispered.

"Yeah, evil," Trevor agreed.

I pulled away from the object and leaned back on the crate in disgust. I felt choked up, like I had something stuck in my throat.

What horrible thing had we opened?

Then I heard new sounds, loud beeping noises like when a truck is backing up. As whatever it was got closer, I could make out the low groan of machinery and the tread of tires.

"Come on, come on," I whispered to Trevor, shooting to my feet. "That could be Crane."

As I rose, I knocked over the bottle of water. Trevor popped to his feet, too, and then the two of us, working together like a pair of surgeons, began that organized scramble to make it look like we had never been there. We were in perfect synch. Trev got the thing back into the crate, then we hurriedly replaced the nails and kicked the loose straw under the shelving, all in perfect ninja silence. We finished just in time, because almost immediately a forklift turned the corner and rolled down the aisle toward us.

The forklift was carrying a large crate. As it moved closer, I noticed something not right about the crate. The top was open and something was sticking out of it. Something with black hair and piercing green eyes. It was Hollis. I could tell he was having the time of his life. Driving the forklift was none other than my good buddy and Hollis's new best friend, Dmitri.

"Hey, you guys," Hollis screamed, his voice echoing intensely off the high ceilings and concrete. "What are you doing here?"

"We've been looking for you," I hollered back.

I did my best to put the soundscape I had just experienced out of my mind. If you're thinking about something, there's a good chance you'll say it out loud, no matter how hard you try to hide it.

Instead of merely stopping the forklift, Dmitri made it do an ultra-slow-motion police skid out. The tires screeched, and the turn was sharp enough to tip Hollis's crate off of the lift. It toppled over clumsily, and Hollis rolled out of it like he was in a movie.

"You guys have got to try this!" he yelled. "Dmitri's going to teach me to drive it, too." He paused and examined us when we didn't match his excitement. "What's a matter with you guys? You seem weird."

"Nothing," I said, but Hollis knew *something* was up.

Until then, Dmitri had been sitting behind the wheel of

the forklift, just staring out stonily and flexing his little muscles. As soon as his name was mentioned, he hoisted his whole body up into the air, kicked his legs out, and hopped out of the forklift with a twist and a backflip.

Trevor and I were stunned. We'd seen almost every kung fu movie ever made, and even we were impressed with his agility and skill, and I didn't see any wires hanging from the ceiling. Dmitri gave a little nod of his head that seemed to say, "Yeah, I'm hot stuff. And I own this place."

"You guys spilled your water," he said, pointing at the dark slick spreading on the gray concrete. "There are no beverages allowed in here."

As I stared at the changing shape of the water, something was starting to come together in my mind.

"It's just water, dude," I said, oddly fascinated by the shifting puddle.

"A rule's a rule," Dmitri said. "There's priceless stuff in here."

I was about to snap back, "Yeah, what about the rule against using the forklift as a bumper car?" but Trevor saved the day.

"We'll clean it up, Dmitri," he said. "What's it to you anyway?"

"This is my job," Dmitri said. "Crane pays me to check up on things."

"Like us?" I asked. Boy, that flew out of my mouth before I could stop it.

"Of course not," Dmitri answered. But for some reason I didn't believe him, not for a minute.

"Don't mind Leo, Dmitri," Hollis said. "He thinks everyone's out to get him. Are you going to stay for dinner, Trevor?"

Trevor checked his watch.

"Oh man. I can't, Hollis. My mom's home tonight."

"They close the hospital or something?" Hollis asked.

Trevor's mom is an emergency room nurse at Flushing Hospital in Queens. She works the night shift and sleeps a lot of the day, so he hardly ever gets to see her.

"They gave her the night off."

"Too bad you can't stay," Hollis said. "Leo is in a way better mood when you're here."

"You don't have to play with Leo," Dmitri chimed in. "I will come to your room and be your friend."

Yeah, I thought. And deliver a full report to Crane.

"Cool," Hollis said as he and Dmitri got back on the forklift and took off down the aisle.

"Let's clean up this water so Little Spy Man doesn't tell Klevko," Trevor said.

I didn't want to clean up the water. I loved looking at its shifting shape and slick black surface. I just stood and watched as its edges turned from deep black to gray and then slowly crept back toward the bottle. It was like watching the spill in reverse. In a part of my mind, I was thinking about how already my former life was slipping from me. How after only a few days away from my old apartment and all of my parents' things, it was harder and harder to remember the life I had experienced there. And like that water on the floor, the longer I was away, the more my memories would turn from vivid color to that fading gray until they were all dried up and forgotten. Forgotten like that cry, that horrible, haunting cry that was stored somewhere in my memory, but was now so faded and remote that I couldn't really recall it.

I knew I had heard that sound before, long ago, from before I had words. It gave me that strange but familiar feeling I always have right before I get sick — the way everything is far away and menacing and not right.

I stared at the shrinking pool of water on the floor. Water! That was it!

"Trev," I blurted. "I just realized where I went when I touched that object. I was in water. The bubbling sounds. The darting movements. Those purple whirlpools in the darkness."

"What would that thing be doing in water?" he asked. "It doesn't look like any instrument you'd use on a boat."

"I don't know. All I know is that it caused something terrible to happen. Something I have to make right. I can't explain it. I *heard* something that needs me."

Trevor wasn't even taking notes. He just nodded.

"You felt it, too?" I asked him.

"I felt *something,* at least I think I did. But I can see it had a big effect on you." Trevor paused. "Leo, you okay man? You're dripping sweat and pale as a ghost."

"I'm not sick, but I'm not okay, either."

I was shivering like mad. Trembling. Even though I was hugging myself, I couldn't get warm.

"You've got to rest, Leezer. You're a mess. We'll figure this out tomorrow."

He guided me to the elevator, and pressed the button to call Klevko. When the elevator arrived, Klevko was inside, but he was not alone. Three huge guys dressed in expensive fur coats and hats were standing behind him, scowling.

"Hullo, boys," Klevko said. "These are Russian friends. But you do not talk now. These men are here to do big business. Come, boys, I will take you downstairs. Russian friends, you wait here on fourth floor and I will return with Crane. The boss will show you what you came to see."

Klevko seemed nervous as we rode down. When we reached the ground floor, he shooed us out impatiently.

"Trevor, go home. Leo, you wait here. I will come back for you after I get Crane. If he is late for Russians, he will roar like polar bear."

"That guy really has a thing for polar bears," Trevor observed as we headed outside into the freezing night air. Two seconds later, Stump pulled up in the limo.

"Step on it, kid," he called out. "I have to be back in time to drop those bums at their hotel." He was chewing on the red straw, so I figured he'd had a tough day.

"Tomorrow we get serious," Trevor said to me as he crawled into the backseat. "Get some rest, man."

All I could do was nod. I was wiped out.

After the limo sped off, I stood outside in the freezing cold. There was no moon and I was surrounded by the stench of salami. Yet my mind wouldn't let go of that horrible object in the crate and what I heard when I touched it. Where had I heard that cry before? What had we let out of that box? Something awful was wrapped up in that thing and it filled me with fear. I knew nothing more, only that I didn't have a choice in what was going to happen next. Everything in my being seemed to be leading me to that terrible contraption in crate number 11910091005122622 on the fourth floor.

CHAPTER 15

Not surprisingly, I didn't sleep well that night. I couldn't relax and when I did fall asleep, fragments of dreams kept jerking me awake. Strange dreams where I was in my old apartment, but it really wasn't my apartment. I had lost something important, and I kept running around tearing open cupboards and drawers, that melody and the painful cry all mixed together and playing somewhere from a speaker. When morning finally came, I was exhausted and wired at the same time, part of my body telling me that I needed more sleep, but another part giving me a strange jittery energy.

I was in a fog all day at school. It was all I could do to keep my eyes open, even if my legs were bouncing like mad under my desk and my mind seemed to be working feverishly on a problem I barely understood, and couldn't put into words.

As soon as school was over, I felt a thousand times better. Just knowing that I was free to start work on finding answers was enough to fill me with energy. I raced down the hall and out the front entrance, searching for Trevor. We had arranged to go to Jeremy's after school. We knew he was the guy who could help us investigate those water sounds. I had to see if I could figure out where . . . or who . . . or what . . . they were coming from.

On the steps, I crashed into Hollis.

"You going to Jeremy's?" he asked me.

"Yeah, I guess." I was trying not to sound too enthusiastic so he wouldn't get any ideas of coming along.

"Great," he said. "I'll go with you. Jeremy is going to show me how to build a theremin. It's this super-cool instrument that some Russian guy made like a hundred years ago — just a metal bar, and you don't even touch it to play it, just wave your arms around it. You'll love it! I told the guys I'm going to write a couple songs on it for our band."

I grimaced. How was I going to get out of this? Hollis picked up on my hesitance.

"You don't want me to go, right?"

"It's not that, Hollis. Trevor and I are working on this project and we need another day or two of privacy, you know?"

"No, I don't know," Hollis fumed. "What's up with you, Leo? You're completely ignoring me. You're hiding something from me, I know it. And now you're hogging Jeremy."

"We're conducting an experiment with some recordings," I said.

"You and your stupid experiments with your stupid recordings," he snapped. "You cut everybody out. Fine, Leo, put on your lame headphones and live in your own little world."

"They're not stupid experiments!" I yelled. I wanted to prove that by telling him what I was working on, but I needed more time. "They're really important experiments. You wouldn't understand."

"There. You're doing it again," he snapped again. "You won't even tell me why they're so important. You're just like Dad, always recording, never making. I'm going home. At least Dmitri is there," he said and stomped off angrily.

"Hollis," I shouted after him. But he didn't turn around.

What a brat, I thought. Calling my experiments stupid. Your little songs are stupid. And while you're playing kung fu fire truck with Dmitri, I'll be doing something important, something you couldn't understand in a million years.

Man, I was fuming.

"Leo, you have to tell him." I spun around and it was Trevor, who had overheard the whole conversation. "He thinks you're lying to him, and you are."

"What do you know, Trev? You don't have a brother."

"Yeah, I don't have a brother, so I can see this clearly. And I'm going to forgive your tone of voice because you're under pressure. That's how good a friend I am."

"Sorry, buddy, I'm just pretty tender today. I feel like I'm gonna go over the edge."

I should have said sorry to Hollis, too. I should have told him about my power. But how do you tell your brother that you hear the world with different ears than he does?

Before going to Jeremy's shop, we had to stop by Trevor's building so he could feed his dad's macaws. Walking by Trevor's house meant getting off at my old subway stop, and passing through my old neighborhood. As I turned up 95th, I felt like it was a lifetime ago that I had been there, even though it had only been a few days. We passed my old apartment, and I saw a moving van parked in front. I wondered what lucky kid was moving into my old room. Ouch, that stung.

When we reached Trevor's building, I waited outside while he ran upstairs. As I stood there warming my hands, I heard someone screaming. It was the hallelujah guy, stumbling down the block and shouting at the top of his lungs. Every now and then, he would twirl his cane wildly and shout, "Hallelujah. God's love shines down on us. Open your eyes, heaven is all around you."

Today was one of his good days. On his bad days he screamed about things like hell and gravel pits and would ask, "Can't you see it's all junk? It's all garbage," and then point and twirl his cane and stare at everybody with his wild-man eyes. He was crazy all right, but I had to respect him. He definitely listened to the little voice in his head. He was coming up the street, wearing black pants pulled up high over his huge gut, and those black medical sneakers with giant rubber soles. He must have noticed me watching him, because right when he was about to pass me, he stopped and spun around toward me. He stared right at me like he recognized me. I know he's crazy, but for a moment he looked completely sane. Then he grabbed my wrist with his hand.

"Our space brother needs your help," he said, holding tighter and tighter to my wrist. "You've got to find him." I stared into the blackness of his eyes. There was something hypnotic about them. . . .

"I will help him," I said.

"Hallelujah!" he screamed, then let go of my wrist, twirled his cane a few times and set off down the street yelling, "Heaven is on every street. On every corner. I love you all!"

Jeremy's shop was crowded, and by crowded, I mean that there was one customer in there. From his accent, I could tell he was Italian, and from the way that both Jeremy and Stinky Steve barely acknowledged us, I knew he was rich. They were playing him all these different records that Jeremy kept behind the counter—the good ones—and after each one, the Italian guy would nod his head jerkily and say, "Good, good bridge. Very funky."

Trevor pulled out his binder and graphing calculator and sat down in the corner the shop to start his advanced-track math homework. I walked over to this one section of records that I love. They're called Folkways Records and that company put out my dad's recordings of different tribes and villages across the world. They also put out what they called field recordings, the kind of stuff I do, only better, where people record what they hear in the world. Like there's one record where they used high-tech microphones to record different insects. Another one is just sounds of the digestive system. My personal favorite was "Sounds of the Junk Yard." My least favorite was "Speech After the Removal of the Larynx." Seriously, someone actually recorded that.

When the Italian guy left with a huge pile of records, we went over to Jeremy and Steve. Jeremy was counting a stack of money.

"Good to see you feeling better," Stinky Steve said. "That was some virus you had."

"Hang in there a minute," Jeremy said. "That guy just paid my rent for the entire month. He's Marco, an opera singer, but he loves funk. Go figure."

"No rush," Trevor said. "The wait gave me a chance to dig into this beta function that's stumping me."

"Well, more power to you," Jeremy said. "I can barely make change here."

"You shouldn't look down on math," Stinky Steve cut in. "Music is just math. Music is made from numbers. Figure out the numbers, figure out the music." He put a hand on Trevor's shoulder. "Right, Trevor?"

Trevor sneezed, and covered his nose with a tissue. But I could tell he was faking. Steve's stench was extra-powerful today.

"Where's Hollis?" Jeremy asked me. "He was supposed to come by."

"He's not feeling well," I stammered. Trevor shot me a disapproving look. I saw that Jeremy noticed it, but he didn't ask about it.

"Well, I was going to build this with him today, but maybe you guys can help him with it." He handed me a large box. "It's a theremin kit."

"Don't forget, Leo," Stinky Steve cut in. "I have your Audograph disc at home. I'll go pick it up right now."

"Why don't you take Trevor with you?" Jeremy said. "I want to have a word with Leo."

"Great," Steve answered. "We can talk about the intersection of math and music."

After the two of them left, Jeremy perched himself on the edge of his desk.

"Leo man, what's up with you?" he said, a tone of genuine concern in his voice. I didn't answer.

"Come on, Leo. Don't act like a kid. I know that Hollis isn't sick. And you got strangely ill after you listened to that disc. And today, something's obviously eating you. As Marvin Gaye said, 'What's going on?'"

"I'm okay, Jeremy. I have good and bad days."

"I know it's tough," he said. "I miss your dad, too."

"I'm working on a sound project, something my dad was working on right before he died. I like working on it—makes me feel like he's still here, kind of. Watching over me."

"Your dad believed that music and sound connected us all, even the living and the dead. Maybe that's why you're feeling him."

I nodded. I loved it that Jeremy knew so much about my dad.

"So how can I help, Leo? I am your official tutor, you know."

"Well, I'm trying to find this strange sound I heard in a recording of his. I'm pretty sure it's something from underwater, though I don't know what."

Just then, someone barged into the store talking loudly on a cell phone. "No cell phones," Jeremy growled at him. The guy grimaced, turned red, and walked right back out.

"Ah, underwater sounds." Jeremy smiled and turned back to me. "Leo, my man, everything we hear is underwater. The fluid in our ears is from our childhood in the ocean, the last little drop of ocean we've got."

He slid off the desk and walked over to a beat-up-looking bin in the corner of the store, perched on top of other beat-up-looking bins.

"You're in luck, actually. A professional marine life study group just went defunct, and I bought all their records. And here they are."

Jeremy picked up the bin and carried it over to his desk, the veins in his neck popping out from the strain. Record collecting doesn't exactly put you in the best shape.

"The mother lode, Leo," he said proudly. "Field recordings of every marine mammal imaginable, tons of new age records of whale songs, and even this one where this guy plays the flute to a killer whale."

The bin of records was packed tight.

"Where do I start?"

"I'd start with the field recordings. You can use that turntable over by the window to listen to the records. There's headphones there, too. You know how to use the record player, right?"

I nodded.

"What are the two rules?"

"Don't touch the record," I said. I had heard that about a thousand times from my dad.

"And what's the second rule?"

I'd never heard of a second rule.

"The second rule, Leo, is don't touch the record."

"Don't touch the record, I got it, jeez," I mock grimaced, just like I used to do with my dad.

"I'm serious, Leo. Your hands are clean? You didn't get a slice on the way over here?"

"They're clean, I swear."

You actually do have to touch the record to play it, but they mean, don't touch the grooves. That's the inside part of the record where the music is. When you put the record on, you're only supposed to touch the edges, where there's no music. Records aren't fragile; they can last for hundreds of years. But they are delicate and easy to scratch, and scratches stay forever.

I lugged the bin over to the corner, where the listening station was. This was going to take a lot of time. If each record had forty minutes of sound and there were about a hundred records, that meant 4,000 minutes of sound to wade through. That could take years. Just then, the bells on the door jingled as Trevor and Stinky Steve came back in.

"Hey, Trevor, how long is 4,000 minutes?"

"Two days, eighteen hours," Trevor said almost as soon as the words left my mouth.

"I love this guy," Stinky Steve said, and patted Trevor on the shoulder. "Leo, I'll leave your disc with Jeremy. Then I'm gonna go to lunch."

"But it's four thirty, Steve," Jeremy said.

"Yeah, but I got up at eleven thirty, so it works for me."

After Steve left, Trevor eyed the stack of records and figured out that I was going to have to listen to all of them.

"I'll help," he offered.

"I have to do this myself, Trev. I'm the only one who can match the sound in my head."

Trevor helped me organize all the records into different groups of species — otters, seals, dolphins, and whales. But after that, there wasn't much he could do to help. I told him he could go home if wanted to, or stay there, whatever he liked.

"Go home?" he said. "Are you kidding? I want to be here if you discover something. I'm in this, too, you know."

"You're a good friend, Trev."

"The best one you'll ever have, Leezer." It was awkward for a minute. We always laughed at those male-bonding moments in movies, when one guy turns to the other and says something lame like "I love you, man." And here we were, pretty close to that moment.

"Get to work, genius," Trevor said, breaking the embarrassing silence.

"I'll see you back on dry land, buddy," I answered as I slipped the headphones on and began to listen.

CHAPTER 16

I kept a list of each and every sea mammal I listened to. Sea otter, elephant seal, harbor seal, gray whale, northern right whale, minke whale, fin whale, blue whale, humpback whale, killer whale, false killer whale, Risso's dolphin, Pacific white-sided dolphin, spinner dolphin, harbor porpoise, beluga, melon-headed whale, Atlantic spotted dolphin, rough-toothed dolphin, hourglass dolphin, dusky dolphin, South African fur seal, New Zealand fur seal, walrus, leopard seal, California sea lion, hooded seal, Caspian seal, dugong, manatee, and the coolest animal in the world, the narwhal.

I could go on. That's not even the half of it.

Every record opened up a new underwater world. Each marine mammal made its own peculiar sound in its own frequency, or pitch. Many of the animals made sounds that were too high for humans to hear. A lot of whales, like the humpback, made sounds so low that they traveled halfway around the ocean. On the back of one of the records, it said scientists guessed that marine mammals made sound for all kinds of reasons — to navigate, to communicate, to detect objects, to frighten other animals or to herd them so they are easy to eat, to disguise their identity. Or maybe for no good reason, just to sing.

Listening to that stack of records, I realized that the ocean truly is a musical place, filled with almost limitless animal symphonies. On one of the album jackets I even read that our loud boats and oil tankers make so much noise that many marine mammals become confused, can't hear their friends, and swim where they aren't supposed to.

As I put on one record after another, being sure not to touch the grooves, I began to suspect that the sound I was looking to match was made by a dolphin. That one noise, of little hands squeaking on glass, sounded a lot like the general sound dolphins make when they're communicating with one another. I had learned in Life Science that although dolphins have good eyesight, it's difficult to see underwater so they use super-high-pitched sounds as sonar. The sounds shoot out from their heads, and when they reach something solid, they echo back to the dolphin so it can make a secret image in its mind of what's out there.

I knew I wasn't listening to actual sonar, because our hearing isn't nearly as good as dolphins and we can't pick up the really high frequencies. But there were some dolphin sounds on the records that sounded similar to what I'd heard. Similar, but still not exactly a match. I never heard anything even resembling the one sound that had so blown me away—the one that little swirl of light made when it was all alone. That cry hadn't sounded like a dolphin, more like a little human-type creature. I couldn't find it anywhere.

By the time I looked up from the record player, it was dark outside, and my ears were red and sweaty from the headphones. Trevor was asleep on the floor and cuddling his math book. Jeremy had his own headphones on and was snapping his fingers in time to whatever he was listening to. And Stinky Steve was nowhere to be seen—though his fragrance was still very much present. I was beat. I stood up and stretched.

"No luck?" Jeremy asked, slipping off his headphones.

I just shook my head.

"You can try again. Hard work always pays off. Come by tomorrow. You'll find it, Leo."

I hated the idea of waiting until the next day. I was haunted by that sound, the sad cry from that little purple swirl of light. You must be losing your mind, Leo. You're one step away from twirling a cane at people and shouting, "Sound is all around us. Open your ears, people! Can't you hear the dolphins crying?"

I was dog-tired, my head swimming with sea life sounds. One second, the strange laser sounds of the Antarctic sea lion would ricochet through my brain, another second, the slow oboe of the humpback whale. I thought that maybe I should try touching that terrible thing in the crate again, just to make sure I really heard what I heard. But I didn't have the courage to make it through that painful experience again.

"Can I throw in my two cents, Leo?" Jeremy left his perch on his desk and came over to my corner.

"Yeah, I need help on this one."

"I've been looking for records a long time," he began. "And I'm pretty good at it. There's one thing I've learned. It may sound bizarre but it isn't."

"So what is it?"

"Records find you, you don't find records."

"I like you, Jeremy, but have to tell you, I think all the dust in here is starting to make you a little nuts."

Jeremy laughed. "I told you it sounds weird, but I've seen it countless times. The record finds you when you're ready to see it and hear it. Here's a true story. A couple of years ago, I got a phone call from a guy who was my best friend when I was seven. It had been twenty years since we last talked. He had bought a house in Maine and invited me up for the weekend. You know, go moose hunting or something."

"How could you shoot a moose?"

"Don't worry, I didn't. A few miles before I got to his house, I saw an old man selling junk by the side of the road. I thought I might buy my friend a housewarming present and pulled off. But the guy only had junk. The most interesting thing he had was a rusted carburetor from a 1953 Buick. But when I lifted up a blanket, I found he also happened to have three records. Two were records you see everywhere, but one, Leo, was a record I had been searching for—for at least ten years. And there it was. At a roadside junk stand in rural Maine. I mean, finding it there was like finding the Holy Grail in a garbage can."

"Whoa. How'd it get there?"

"I had no idea. I wondered how many times that had just floated around the world like driftwood? I couldn't understand it, so I did some research. I learned that it had been in Montana, New Jersey, Japan, Vermont, and Maine—passing each time through different hands. Until it wound up at a junk stand in Maine, a junk stand that I just happened to be driving by on the way to see an old friend, an old friend who I hadn't talked to in years. Now you tell me, Leo. Would you say that I found that record, or that it found me?"

"It definitely found you."

"Exactly. Things find you when you're ready to receive them. And not just records, either."

Did that mean I might have to take a random trip to visit a long-lost friend? Or wait seven years for another package from my dad?

"How do I get records to find me, Jeremy?"

"I think you have to try to see the world with fresh eyes. Every time you look at something, you have to really look at it, like you were a baby. Most people are so caught up in their heads worrying about their problems, they don't see what's right in front of them. I knew a guy who searched all over the world for a record and didn't realize that it was already in his collection."

I was interested in what Jeremy was saying, but frankly, I didn't quite get how it applied to me. Jeremy noticed, and gave it one more shot.

"Leo, I'm saying that you have to pay attention. Listen to your emotions and instincts. I didn't find that record because I was looking for it, I found that record because I was *looking*."

I understood why Jeremy and my dad were such good friends. My dad had told me almost the exact same thing in his letter — to listen to that little voice inside of me. Suddenly, I felt like crying. Jeremy was great, but he wasn't my dad. I missed him so much. I ached to see him, to hear him call me Leezer or even to hear his voice, to touch him, to give him one more hug. But he wasn't there. The only thing I could touch was one of the records he'd made. That was as close as I was going to get.

I walked over to the Folkways section. I flipped through *Sounds of Insects, Sounds of the Junk Yard, Sounds of People Without Voice Boxes*. Right after that one, and I couldn't believe this, there was a field recording called *Sounds and Ultra-Sounds of the Bottle-Nose Dolphin*.

It was the only dolphin record in the whole store that I hadn't listened to yet. I held it above my head.

I tried not to get my hopes up, but somehow I knew that this was the one. I knew it just by the way it felt in my hand. I put the headphones on my sweaty, red ears and listened.

Side one started with some guy named Jay Lylo talking. He was a dolphin scientist, and rattled off a lot of dolphin facts. Then he played an underwater soundscape he had recorded. I recognized the firefly sounds, the ones that sounded like frying bacon. They were exactly what I had heard. He explained that they were snapping shrimp. I skipped around to the next section and put the needle down. It was those little squeaky sounds — the human hands on glass — an identical match to what I'd heard.

I was so excited, my hands were shaking. But still, what I wanted to hear most was the almost human cry of the purple swirl of light. I felt like it was calling me. Urgently.

I flipped the record over to side two, and that's when things got weird. Lylo explained that he had been trying to decode dolphin language and had spent years trying to get them to speak like humans. He said that he trained some dolphins to make vowel sounds and syllables out of their blowholes, sounds that they could control, sounds that humans could hear, so that if dolphins had language, they could eventually speak in a way humans could hear.

And then he played those sounds. Strange, almost human sounds. There it was. I heard it. The cry. The anguish. Just like my purple swirl.

"It found me, Jeremy. I'm serious. It found me!"

He just smiled and shrugged. I swear, the guy was Yoda. I'd found it. I'd found it. I'd found it.

But there was more.

The record had one final track. And it contained something I was totally unprepared for.

CHAPTER 17

The record crackled as it switched bands, and then I heard a voice. That's when I stopped breathing.

"Hello. This is Kirk Lomax, PhD candidate in ethnomusicology at Columbia University and field recordist with Folkways Records."

It was him, my dad, sounding as if he were right there in the room with me. Alive and well. As I listened to his voice, I clung to every word, every syllable, as if hearing him would bring him back to me.

"Several months ago, I received a remarkable letter from Dr. Jay Lylo at the Communications Research Institute in Miami, Florida. In it, Dr. Lylo described his research with bottlenose dolphins in the hopes of one day communicating intelligently with these creatures. While performing his experiments, Dr. Lylo kept his seven dolphin subjects in separate compartments. This separation meant they could not communicate using their sonar or ultrasonic vocalizations. To his amazement, Dr. Lylo observed that these dolphins developed a new means of communication. They were exchanging sounds with one another from their blowholes. Some of these conversations lasted over an hour.

"Dr. Lylo said that when he first heard these communications he was overcome with emotion. The communications affected him on a musical level. For the first time, he was able to hear and truly feel the complex emotional lives of the dolphins. Dr. Lylo invited me to the Research Institute to observe and record.

"I spent several weeks at the Institute recording hundreds of hours of these fascinating communications. Dr. Lylo and I have chosen one episode that we feel demonstrates the sonic range, complexity, and emotions of these intelligent creatures. It is my view that we should now welcome a new tribe into our human family — the seven research dolphins at the Communications Research Institute. We have named the recording you will now hear 'Isolation Blues.'"

Before I could catch my breath, I heard one of those cries. That was *it*, the sound, the one that came to me from the contraption in the crate. The one that had been haunting me. It quivered and warbled in the air. In it, I could hear and feel pain. It was unsteady and unnatural, like a dog trying to walk on two legs. It sounded like a child's desperate cry.

It wasn't just a simple sound. It was complex, made up of short sounds and long calls, rising and falling. I heard emotions in it: frustration, sadness, a desire to hear someone respond. And something did. Another dolphin answered.

The sounds of its artificial voice vibrated painfully in the air. They were communicating. And then another dolphin, and another, and another. With my eyes closed, I saw them in my mind. They were all talking to one another, and I could tell they were also listening. At first they were happy just to be hearing one another, but soon the whole thing took a sad turn. I could hear in the voices their intelligence, creativity, emotions. They longed to be somewhere else. They wanted to move around, jump in the air, be free in the water. No, this wasn't a bird chirping — these animals had souls: They had thoughts and feelings and desires and complicated needs. They were sick in those compartments.

As I listened and concentrated, a powerful wave of recollection overtook me and I remembered where I had heard those sounds before. Suddenly, I wasn't in Jeremy's record store anymore. The sounds took me back to my bed at our old apartment. I was three years old.

I had the blankets wrapped around me and pulled up to my chin, but I was still so cold and shivering. It was nighttime. I had been in this bed for so long. I was sick, real sick. My ears were throbbing. Mom would come in and check on me with a worried look on her face, but she was so busy with Hollis, and she couldn't stay with me. I'd hear Hollis crying, and hear her talking to my dad about me. But mostly I heard those terrible sounds. I had heard Dad say they were dolphin sounds but I didn't know what a dolphin was. Was it a ghost? A monster? It had to be to make such terrifying noises.

They flooded the entire apartment, and made me so scared. When I slept, I heard them, and I dreamed of strange, contorted humanlike things crying in pain. I'd wake up to them, hearing them through the walls in the next room. I was too weak to get out of bed. I couldn't move. And I was alone with those sounds for so long, shivering, but with such a high fever that every one of those sounds throbbed in my eardrums. Why wasn't Dad coming in to check on me? Where was he?

"Daddy!" I screamed as loud as I could and leapt out of bed, running for the closed door. "Daddy, where are you?"

I slammed into something hard in front of me and I crashed to the floor. "Ow, ow, ow!" I was bawling. I heard footsteps race toward my door, and as it flung open, those strange sounds filled my entire room. He was in my doorway. "Daddy, make it stop, make it stop." He was at my side, and holding me.

"You're okay, Leo. You're okay. I'm here."

"Make it stop, make it stop. Please!" I was trembling and shivering.

"Make what stop?"

"The monsters! Make them stop."

"Okay, Leo, you stay here, I'll be right back."

"Don't leave me."

"I'll be right back, I promise."

He ran out the door, and in an instant the sounds were gone. He was back in my room, in his robe and slippers. He turned on the night-light and sat on the floor by me, and rubbed my back as I gasped and cried. "It's okay, buddy," he kept saying. "It was just the tape recorder. There aren't any monsters."

When I had stopped crying, he got me back in bed, and laid down beside me.

"I'm so sorry," he kept saying. "Just daddy's work. You're okay."

With my head on his chest, he kept telling me everything was okay and rubbing my back until my breathing got back to normal and I calmed down. I was so warm and calm, and I felt his heart beating in his chest through my whole body for what felt like forever. *Bump, babump, babump.*

I pulled off the headphones and opened my eyes and felt the memory quieting down in my head. I realized I was safe, in Jeremy's record store. In front of me, the shiny vinyl record was spinning around and around. It was over, and the needle was at the end in the run-out groove, just going over this same bump every rotation. *Bump, babump, babump.* My entire face was wet with tears, but at least I understood. I knew why that sound filled me with terror. It was the sound of Lylo's dolphins, of my dad editing their recordings I had just heard. Hearing those cries again threw me back to my little self, to that horrible night when my dad was there to comfort me. The sad truth was that now I was alone, with no one to make that sound in my head go away.

I stopped the turntable and took a deep breath. Trevor was awake, and both he and Jeremy were just staring sadly at me. When I made eye contact with Trevor, he nervously looked away. I took the record off the turntable and put it back in its jacket.

"I was just . . . " I started. "Those dolphins are . . . " I felt a lump in my throat and my eyes started to water again. "I think, um . . . " I tried to blink away the water. "They reminded me of . . . " The water was leaking out of my eyes now. "I'm . . . uh . . . just a second . . . " I felt my face and neck twitching. I tried to talk again, but my whole face contorted. I couldn't control it anymore. And it all streamed out. I was so embarrassed. I wanted to stop, but the harder I tried, the more it came out.

"It's okay, Leo," I heard Jeremy say. "It's okay, just let it out."

Then I felt a hand on my back.

"You're okay, Leezer," Trevor said.

And then they let me cry for what felt like forever.

CHAPTER 18

After the waterworks, Jeremy thought it'd be a good idea to get out of the store and go to the diner down the street, and maybe get a milkshake. He could get a milkshake, but I was going to get a cheeseburger deluxe. I was feeling a lot better, and very hungry.

The diner was just up the block, and though the place was a bit of a dive, and the cheeseburger was only average, it felt great to be eating a meal while sitting down.

"So, Jeremy," I started, as the waiter took away our greasy plates. "What do you know about that guy who made that dolphin record, Jay Lylo? Think he's still alive?"

"I would have heard if he wasn't," Jeremy said, gulping down the last of his second milkshake. "He's famous, you know. Pretty much the father of a whole generation of dolphin researchers."

"How can I talk to him?"

"Gosh, Leo, I don't know. He was supposed to speak at one of your dad's classes last year, but he was a no-show. A guy in my class said that he went a little bonkers. Not unusual in geniuses."

"But there's gotta be a way to find him," I said. "This project that Trevor and I are working on, there's just so many things I need to understand. My dad would have —"

"Hold on, I think I know a guy," Jeremy said. He always knew a guy.

Jeremy pulled out his cell phone and scrolled through his numbers.

"No cell phones!" a waiter screamed from across the diner.

"I have the same policy myself," Jeremy said. "I'll be right back, fellas," and he stepped outside into the icy rain. While he was gone, I told Trevor about finding the sound I was looking for on Lylo's album.

"You don't think this Lylo character was involved with . . . " Trevor lowered his voice. ". . . that device?"

"I don't think so. I can't see my dad working with someone who would be."

Unlike his stepbrother, I thought.

Crane said he knew what was in each and every crate. He called them his babies. He selected everything in his warehouse with care. He must have sought out that device. Who knew, maybe he had spent years searching for it, just like Jeremy and that record?

"But maybe Lylo knows something about it?" Trevor asked.

"He must. I just feel like he's connected to all this stuff. And I don't just mean that device. I mean all of it. The blue disc, my power, the dolphins, my parents, that island, that—" Trevor was shooting me a look that said be quiet.

"Okay, Leo," Jeremy said as he slid back into the booth, still shivering a bit. "The call has gone out."

"You found him?"

"Sort of. I left him a message."

"That's great news. When can I talk to him?"

"That might take awhile. He's on a small island somewhere in the South Pacific. Started some kind of dolphin reserve for former show dolphins."

"When do you think we'll hear from him?"

Jeremy shrugged. "From what my friend told me, he only lets himself be found when he wants to be found."

"How long will that take, Jeremy? A week, a month, a year?" The thought of even waiting a week made me queasy.

"What you need comes to you," he answered in a typical Jeremy way.

When we went outside, snow was fluttering lightly in huge, fluffy crystals. The streets were covered in a razor-thin blanket of white snow. It wouldn't stick for long, but that was okay. Trevor caught a big flake on his glove, and just stared at it for a moment, smiling to himself.

Jeremy gave us forty dollars from the Italian opera singer's money for the cab ride home. It was dark, and he didn't want us taking the subway. He said that he'd call if he heard from Jay Lylo.

The cab dropped Trevor off at his building, then headed downtown over to the Queensboro Bridge. As we crossed the bridge, I realized that Manhattan was starting to feel a lot less like home. I was eager to get back to the warehouse, to see Hollis and give him his theremin kit. And to make up with him for the hundredth time this week. He was getting an unfair break from me, and I knew it.

When the car pulled up to the warehouse, the driver told me it cost thirty-six bucks. I was hoping to keep the change. Crane had made sure that we had everything we needed, but he wasn't exactly loose with walk-around money. But I gave the four dollars as a tip to the driver. His name was Oscar, and the whole ride he'd bobbed his head to an unheard rhythm. I liked Oscar.

I lugged the theremin kit into the lobby. I rang the bell for the elevator, but it took over five minutes for Klevko to get there. I wished he'd just teach me how to work it myself. If Dmitri could, why couldn't I?

Klevko picked me up, but instead of taking me to the penthouse, he stopped the elevator at the fourth floor.

"Why are we stopping here?"

"Crane, he tells me to bring you to here. He wants to talk to you about something important."

Crane was waiting as the elevator door slid open, looking none too happy, I might add.

"Accompany me, Leo," he said. "There is something I'd like to show you."

There it was. I was toast and I knew it. As we walked down the aisle, I knew where Crane was leading me — to the crate we had broken into. I tried desperately to come up with a story to explain why I had been snooping in his things when he'd explicitly told me not to. I half wanted to run and hide, but Klevko was nipping at my heels like the watchdog he was paid to be.

"This is the crate in question," Crane said, pointing to the one Trevor and I had pried open. I was just about to launch into a confession of some kind, when he held up his hand.

"Leo, please don't interrupt me when I'm speaking to my employees."

To my surprise, he turned to Klevko. "Klevko, see that this crate is ready to be shipped Saturday. The Russians will come to pick it up at exactly six in the morning, and I told them we would have it ready on the wharf. I don't want anything bungled this time. Do you think you can handle that, Klevko?"

"What's in there, Uncle Crane?" I asked. Maybe he would shed some light on what that thing was.

"None of your business, young man," he answered. "But I will tell you this. It's something the Russians paid a pretty penny for. As your brother Hollis would say, enough to buy a yacht."

Crane threw back his head and laughed. As he did, he put his left hand on my shoulder. His right hand was still touching the crate. Suddenly, I felt a powerful vibration run through me, then a bolt of electricity. The light started to shimmer in front of my eyes, and the low humming began, followed by the popping sound of bacon frying.

Oh no. Not here. Not now. Not in front of Crane!

I felt like a huge magnet was pulling me toward that crate, toward the horrible object inside it. I could feel its evil pull and hear its bubbling noises even though Crane's body was separating us. I felt myself slipping into the trance. I had to fight it with every shred of my being. I had to stop it. Crane could never know my secret.

I resisted with my mind and my body. Do not go there, I chanted to myself. Do not go there. Stay away, purple swirl. I do not see you. I do not hear you. I tried to reach out to take Crane's hand off my shoulder, to cut the connection to the crate, but I was too weak, too hypnotized to move.

Just as I was slipping deeper into the trance, I heard Crane yell, "Klevko, you fool!" He removed his hand from my shoulder and paced angrily over to Klevko.

"Rats!" he boomed. "I just saw two rats scampering down this aisle! I thought I had entrusted the extermination to you. And look what your incompetence has given me — filthy rodents among my priceless possessions."

Now that Crane's hand was off me, I felt my own strength returning. I inched away from the crate, away from its power.

"I am sorry," Klevko said. "I will call the men right now. I will take care of everything. No more rats, you will see."

"Klevko, you donkey, if you can't take care of the rats, how can I trust you to take care of the Russian package?"

Klevko reached for a handkerchief to wipe away the beads of sweat that had popped out on his forehead and hurried away to call the exterminators. He moved fast to get out of the range of Crane's wrath.

Then Crane turned to me. I had moved down the aisle, trying to keep away from the dolphin crate. My mind was racing, thinking about what I had heard . . . the news that the crate was being shipped out in less than forty-eight hours.

"What I came here to show you, Leo," Crane said, ignoring his meltdown with Klevko as though nothing had happened, "was an object that . . . shall we say . . . I reclaimed from your father's possessions when packing up your former apartment. I thought you could tell me something about it."

He walked down the aisle, stopping at a small crate the size of a basketball. As he opened it, my phone went off. It was Jeremy, so I inched away from Crane.

"I have good news and bad news," Jeremy said, talking a mile a minute. "The good news — I found Lylo. Amazing. He called immediately when he got my message. Said to tell you he's so sorry about your dad. Says he loved him and is glad to help you in any way."

I watched Crane reach into the crate and carefully remove an object wrapped in a dirty burlap bag with a rope drawstring at the top.

"What's the bad news?" I whispered.

"Says he can't talk to you about the dolphins on the phone. Has to be a face-to-face. Claims the Russian government has been tapping his phone for years. Sounds like the guy might truly have gone off the deep end."

Wait a minute.

The Russians? Hadn't Crane just said that the crate with the contraption was being delivered to the Russians? Maybe there was some connection. Maybe Lylo wasn't bonkers.

"Leo," Crane said sternly, "put that phone away. It's common courtesy not to take a call in the middle of a conversation."

"But you do it all the time," I said.

"I do it for business," Crane answered. "When large sums of money are involved, common courtesy does not apply."

"I gotta go," I said to Jeremy.

"Just one more thing," he said. "The bad news is that Lylo is at his reserve in the South Pacific and has no plans to come here until the summer. So sounds like you have to chill out until then."

"We'll talk," I said to Jeremy. "Bye."

Crane reached out and took my phone. He turned it off and placed it in his jacket pocket, right behind his gray silk scarf.

"In the future, Leo, please turn off your mobile device when we are together," he said. "I won't have you multitasking in my company. Now, I'd like you to concentrate on this."

Crane placed the burlap bag on top of one of the crates. Chunks of dried red mud fell off as he untied the drawstring and lifted out a mask made of a golden-colored wood. The eyes were hollow and the teeth were sharp, and grotesque ears as big as a human fist stuck out from each side of the face. I remembered my father showing me that mask when he returned from a trip to Borneo. He said it was what they called a soul-catcher mask and had been given to him by a tribal chief in a remote village by a wild river.

"Do you recognize this?" Crane asked me.

"Yeah, my dad got it in Borneo from an old chief."

Crane's eyes lit up.

"Borneo? Did he happen to mention if it was in Long Pulung?"

"Maybe. I'm not sure."

A very irritated look crossed Crane's face.

"Leo, do you see where this mask has been split, down here at the bottom? I think it's possible that this is part of a long-lost twin mask, perhaps even one of the legendary twin masks of Long Pulung."

"So if that's what it is, it would be worth a ton of money, right?"

"More than you can imagine, Leo. So you see why it's so important that you search your memory for any details your father told you about that trip."

I actually did remember some more details about the trip. About the ten-day boat ride into the jungle and the danger-ous rapids they had to cross to reach the village.

I knew Crane wanted that information, and wanted it bad. But he had something I wanted just as bad. A plane. A private jet. To take me to the South Pacific.

It was an outrageous idea, a wild thought that came to me in a stroke of genius as I listened to Crane describe the fortune he could make from this mask. He would probably say no, but I had nothing to lose.

"Uncle Crane," I said, "I do know some things about that mask. But I promised my dad I'd keep what he told me a secret."

"You can share your secrets with me, Leo. I am to be trusted."

"If I tell you, will you help me with something?"

"Yes, of course, my boy. I am here to help you."

"It's kind of a big favor to ask."

"Well, if the information you give me about this mask can set me on the right course, then I owe you a big favor in return. That's the way business works, Leo. One hand washes the other."

I took a deep breath and plunged in.

"I'd like to borrow your plane."

"My plane?" Crane deadpanned.

"See, my friend Trevor is a really brilliant scientist and he and I are doing a science project. We think it could win a national science championship or something. But we need to visit the lab of this famous scientist, so I was thinking, maybe we can borrow your plane?"

"And where does this scientist live?"

"In the South Pacific. On an island."

"The South Pacific?" Crane threw his head back and laughed. "Out of the question, Leo. What could you possibly be studying that would require you to see a man halfway around the world?"

"Dolphins," I said.

Ever so slightly I saw one of his cheek muscles twitch.

"Dolphins, eh? Fascinating creatures. I have an interest in them myself. And when do you need this plane?"

"As soon as possible." Then, remembering the Russians, I added, "Before Saturday."

Crane pulled out his phone and called up a calendar on the screen. He squinted at the dates, chewing his bottom lip.

"Actually, the jet is scheduled to make a delivery to Singapore over the weekend. I suppose I could arrange for it to make a stop. That is, if you tell me what I need to know about this mask. A favor for a favor, Leo."

"Okay. I know that the shaman who gave it to my dad said it was a soul-catcher mask."

"Right. Right. That's very typical of the region. Go on."

"And the village where the shaman lived was at the end of a long river."

"Yes. That could be the Kayan. Or the Bahau."

"And my dad had to go through really rough rapids to get there."

"Yes. Yes. Long Pulung is said to be situated above a bend in the river where there are many dangerous rapids."

Crane was starting to breathe fast, and I thought I saw his hands shaking a bit.

"Leo, do you realize what you're saying? This mask could be it! The real thing. I will commission an archaeological study right away."

"And what about the plane?"

"A deal is a deal. Tomorrow is Friday. You may leave at sunrise on Saturday. You have the weekend to do your research. I'll expect you here for breakfast on Tuesday morning."

My heart jumped in my chest, but I kept my cool.

"There is one very important condition," Crane said. "I must stay here to begin the investigation of the twin mask, so I will not be able to go with you. Obviously, you will need appropriate adult supervision."

"I think I know someone."

But Crane wasn't listening. He was already examining the fanglike teeth of the mask and smiling his greedy little smile.

CHAPTER 19

s I rode the elevator back up to the penthouse, my head was spinning. I could hardly believe what had just happened. We were going to the South Pacific to visit Jay Lylo. That is, if I could get Jeremy to go with me, and Trevor's parents to say yes. Those were two big ifs. I reached for my cell phone to call them both, but it was gone. Right, Crane had taken it from me. I was going to have to borrow Hollis's.

Hollis. What was I going to tell Hollis? I went over several possibilities in my mind. I could tell him the whole truth and just let him handle it. But then I thought it might freak him out and in his panic, he'd tell his new friend Dmitri about it, Dmitri could report it to Crane, and then the whole deal would be up.

Hollis's door was shut, but I barged right in anyway. He was sitting on his bed, writing notes on some sheet music. Some very peaceful violin music was playing.

"Hey, chief," I said, opening the door and shoving the theremin kit at him. "Jeremy sent this for you. I thought we could build it together, just the brothers."

Hollis looked pleased to get the theremin, but not so pleased to see me. "Listen, Leo, I don't know what you're trying to do," he said. "So leave the kit and keep your brotherly gestures to yourself."

"You know what, Hollis, you're right. And I'm sorry. For a lot of things. I haven't been a good brother these last few days. I want to make it up to you. So let's build this thing, okay?"

Hollis still had his head buried in his sheet music, but I could see the slightest little smile curl on his lips and the feel of the room began to lighten.

"Leo, you had to wear Velcro shoes until you were ten, how are you going to put that thing together?"

"It can't be that hard. Besides, I wore Velcro shoes because they were cool, not because I couldn't tie my laces."

"You still can't tie your laces, bro."

I looked down at my sneakers, and he was sort of right. I had had the same knots in them for months. We both laughed. As we laughed, I remembered it was Mom who had tied those knots.

"Is this Mom's music?" I asked.

"Yeah, I'm writing these songs, but they're all missing something, a certain sound. I wanted to . . ." he trailed off.

"Come on," I said, sitting down on the floor of his room. "Jeremy said this thing was easy to put together."

It turned out to be very easy. We didn't even need the instruction manual. The completed theremin was supposed to look like a small metal antenna sticking out of a wood base. We screwed the wood base together and connected all the wires, circuit boards, and the speaker together.

When we finished it, Hollis tried it out. All he had to do was move his hand near the metal antenna and the instrument made an alien noise, somewhere between that woman who plays the electric saw on the subway platform and a soprano opera singer.

It took Hollis only a few minutes before he was doing amazing things on it, going from Beethoven to Stevie Wonder. As I listened, I thought about our talents. I got my dad's interest in music and sound, but when it came to the ability to make music, Hollis got our mom's gift. My sound-bending power was turning out to be pretty magical, but Hollis had a gift, too, and his was absolutely real.

"Can I borrow your phone?" I asked him, getting to my feet.

He tossed it to me, and as I went to leave, he said, "This thing is so cool. It's going to be perfect for my new garage band, the Freight Elevators. We just got picked to play at the school dance on Saturday."

I stopped dead in my tracks.

"This Saturday? As in the day after tomorrow?"

"Yeah, we're gonna shred. Man, thanks, Leo. This is perfect!"

"No problem," I said stonily, but my mind was reeling. This Saturday! I won't be here this Saturday.

How was I going to tell that to Hollis? He was going to be really pissed.

Face it, Leo, I thought as I made a beeline for my room. You're a lousy brother. I promised myself I'd make it up to him when I got back. By then, maybe I'd understand more and could share it with him. At least, that's what I hoped.

I called Trevor and gave him the news about the plane.

"You have to ask your mom and dad tonight," I instructed him. "Tell them it's for our science project and my uncle Crane is supervising the whole thing. That we'd only miss one day of school. All that stuff."

Then I called Jeremy.

"You have to come," I told him. "It's the only way Crane will let us go."

"Ease up there, fella, I have a business to run."

"You can let Stinky Steve take over for a couple of days."

"Oh yeah, there's a comforting thought. The customers would have to come find him in the bathroom."

"Jeremy," I pleaded, "what would my dad do in this situation? What did he always say?"

"He said, 'Follow your curiosity. All true learning is the result of asking questions.'"

"Right. So that's what I'm doing."

"Okay, kiddo. If you put it that way, how can I say no? But I'm warning you, if Stinky Steve breaks my toilet again, you're paying for it."

I had done it. The plans were in motion.

▤ ▤ ▤

When Stump dropped us off at school the next morning, Hollis ran off to no doubt tell his bandmates about their new instrument. I waited on the front steps and called Jeremy.

"Are you going for sure?" I asked him.

"Against my better judgment. What about Trevor?"

"He's supposed to be working it out with his parents."

"So I guess I should call Lylo. He's going to be one mighty surprised scientist."

"Listen, Jeremy, I know this is crazy."

"Yes, it is." He paused, then he said, "Leo, you've got a lot of your dad in you. And I just want to say, as your tutor, I approve."

Then he hung up.

Trevor was waiting for me inside the front hallway. He was pacing back and forth, and burst into a huge smile when he saw me.

"You get the go-ahead?" I said, bounding up to him.

"My dad's okay with it, but he's clearing it with my mom this morning. He wants phone numbers, itineraries, information on everybody and everything involved. And he wants to talk to someone in charge."

"We'll give him Jeremy's phone number. He'll seal the deal."

I suspected Trevor's dad would say yes. He's a lot like my dad in that he believes the best school is real-life experience.

At lunch, Trevor called his dad and got the final okay. The trip was on.

We agreed he'd get to the warehouse early the next morning so we could go to the fourth floor and take the contraption. There was no use going all the way to the South Pacific if we couldn't show the real thing to Lylo. We planned that Trevor would put it in his duffel and we'd hide it way back in the plane so I wasn't too near it. We'd put another crate in its place, and by the time Klevko or the Russians discovered the device wasn't inside, we'd be on our way to the South Pacific. We congratulated ourselves on devising the perfect plan.

Perfect except for Hollis. When I told him, he didn't even look at me. Just turned around and walked away.

It was just me and Stump in the limo on the ride home. I asked if I could sit up in the front seat with him. When he noticed how preoccupied I seemed, he asked if I still had the straw.

"Yeah," I said, "but I got some problems the straw can't fix."

"It doesn't do everything. Don't be a lunatic. It helps, that's all."

"I've got something important to do, Stump. But I don't know if I'm up to it."

"What are you, kiddo? Twelve? Eleven?"

"I'm thirteen," I said, adding some fake bass to my voice.

"Thirteen. That's the age when things get tough. All over the world, kids your age have to go through a *waddyacallit*, a rite of passage. Where you face your fears. To see what you're made of, test your mettle, you know? They say that's the age a boy becomes a man."

"It's not easy turning thirteen, Stump. I have some issues."

"What are you, some kind of two-bit head shrinker?

Issues are for wimps. Whatever it is you're going through, just show 'em you're tough, even if you're scared, got me?"

"Sure, Stump."

I couldn't believe it. Here I was, taking advice from Stump. Not even a week ago, that guy scared me to death. Now he was like my personal counselor.

That night, Crane was meeting with an anthropologist about the mask, but he did leave me a warm and cuddly note that said,

> YOUR PLANE IS ORDERED.
> BE READY TO LEAVE AT FIVE A.M.
> DON'T DO ANYTHING FOOLISH.
> YOURS, CRANE RATHBONE

The guy was all heart. But I wasn't complaining. He did make good on our deal.

I set my alarm for three thirty in the morning. Trevor was supposed to arrive at four so we could swap the crates before anyone was up. I don't think I even closed my eyes that night.

By four I was dressed and packed and headed for the elevator to pick up Trevor. The elevator was actually easy to operate, and I didn't lose a finger.

He was waiting for me at the building entrance, a huge duffel bag slung over his shoulder.

"Don't even ask what time I had to wake up," he whispered. "Three subways plus a thirty-minute walk. Man, it smells like a bad deli around here."

I had learned that Finkelstein's factory did most of their work at night, and every morning, the entire neighborhood smelled like a salami on rye, hold the mustard.

Trevor got in the elevator and I took us to the fourth floor. Quietly, we crept over to the aisle that contained our crate. I didn't want to get near it, so I sent Trevor to see that it was the right one.

"Make sure you double-check the number," I whispered. "It's 11910091005122622. Don't mess up."

I really didn't have to say that. Trevor was a whiz at numbers, and he probably had it memorized as soon as I said it.

"This is it," he said and lifted off the top. "I'm going to take it out now. You ready?"

"Put something in its place."

Trevor found a similar crate a few feet down. He slid the top off and took out a ceramic figure of what looked like a Chinese warrior and carefully put it in the crate in place of the device.

Suddenly, we heard a noise. Footsteps. Was it Klevko? Dmitri? Or worse, Crane? My blood froze in my veins.

"What should I do?" Trevor whispered.

"Don't move. Not a muscle."

The footsteps came a little closer, then stopped. They were in the next aisle. Remembering Stump's advice — to never show them that you're afraid even if you are — I gathered all my courage and crept over to the next aisle. Staring up at me were the glowing eyes of a large rodent. Not a rat, but an opossum. It was an ugly creature, the size of a dog with the look of a rat.

The opossum wasn't all that thrilled to meet me there in the dark, and he scampered off as quickly as he'd come. Trevor put the dolphin device into his duffel bag, and put the lids back on both crates. Then, keeping as silent as we could, we ran back to the elevator, got off on the penthouse floor, and bolted to my room. When we were inside with the door locked, he took the contraption out of his duffel to wrap it more carefully.

"I had forgotten what a horrible thing this is," he said, shaking his head in disbelief. "It looks like a torture device."

"I think I've figured out what it could be." I had been thinking about nothing but that device for days. "I bet it's a helmet. Check out the straps and the buckle. And the shape is just like a dolphin's head. Especially the bottlenose."

"What about the pins?" Trevor asked.

I could barely speak the words. "Maybe they're to hold the helmet on. Maybe to reach its brain. Who knows?"

I felt nauseous at the thought of someone strapping that device onto the head of an innocent dolphin. It was a shocking and disgusting thought. A shameful thing to do. Maybe those Russians who were buying it knew how it was used. And maybe that's why they were willing to pay such a high price for it — to hide their shame.

Trevor covered the dolphin helmet with his clothes and slipped it back into his duffel. An hour later, when Crane came to get us, we were waiting for him in the hall, looking like two bright-eyed science guys, eager to conduct their research.

And in a way, that's exactly what we were.

CHAPTER 20

When we left the building, it was still dark out. And just like that morning less than a week ago, the steaming black limousine was waiting outside in the predawn gloom, with Stump leaning against it, munching on his red straw. The only sound was the occasional chirp of morning birds . . . and the scampering of little feet behind us.

"I'll help you with your bag, Trevor."

It was Dmitri. What was he doing up at this hour of the morning, I wondered.

"Thanks, Dmitri, we're fine," Trevor said. But Dmitri grabbed on to the handle anyway.

"Dmitri," I said in my adult voice. "This is not your bag. Leave it alone."

"I'm just being friendly," he pouted, looking down at his shoes.

I hesitated for just a second because he was acting so pathetic and in that instant, he grabbed the bag from Trevor and disappeared behind the car. I heard the mini-flashlight he kept on his duffel bag clunking against the zipper. Dmitri was opening it! That low down sneak. *I knew it.* I dashed around the car but Stump was already there, yanking the bag out of Dmitri's hands.

"Hey, punk. Gimme that." Stump didn't like anyone interfering with his job. He chased Dmitri around the limo and shooed him away.

"Mind your own business for a change," he said to Dmitri, tossing the bag in the trunk and slamming it shut. I tried to see if the duffel was unzipped at all, but I couldn't tell for sure, and Stump was already holding open the door and telling us to get in. You don't argue with Stump.

We picked up Jeremy at his apartment, then sped along dark, empty roads to the Brooklyn-Queens Expressway. Looking across the East River, I could just barely make out the faint silhouette of the Statue of Liberty, and behind that, the first orange hints of the rising sun. Nobody said a word the whole drive. I didn't trust myself to speak, I was so afraid I'd reveal something about our mission. When we reached the airport, our car entered a private gate and we drove right up to the tarmac toward the private jet.

We walked up the stairs to the plane and each crew member said, "Good morning, sir," as we passed. I touched the outside of the airplane right before we went in — not to use my power — it was just something my mom did every time we flew. She said it was for good luck. I couldn't help but wonder if she had touched the plane for good luck on their sightseeing flight over Antarctica. Maybe she forgot. Maybe that's why they crashed. I knew it was a silly, superstitious thing to think, but I couldn't stop my mind from going there and it hurt.

Inside, it was warm and beige. A woman in a perfect flight attendant outfit, perfect makeup, and a perfect fancy hat perched on her perfect hair, greeted us.

"Good morning, gentlemen. I'm Susan and I'll be your personal server on the flight. This way to your seats."

These weren't regular airplane seats. They were more like huge, comfy La-Z-Boy chairs. It was a small plane and there were perhaps ten seats scattered throughout the cabin. Each chair had a TV, a table, pillows and blankets, and a remote that controlled the window curtains, the video screen, and your footrest. Susan seated us in the middle of the cabin, right across the aisle from each other. I kneeled on my seat and took a peek around. Directly behind my seat, Jeremy was sitting nervously and digging his fingernails into the armrest.

"You don't look so good, Jeremy."

"The only thing I like worse than getting up early is flying," he said, picking up the emergency pamphlet. "Twenty hours. Oh boy."

I'd never had a problem with flying before, but I found myself scanning the cabin for all the emergency exits. I wondered if I'd ever be able to fly again without fear.

I had thought it was just us three on the plane, until I noticed a large man in the back, dressed in a shiny black suit. He was sitting absolutely still with his hands on a brief-case in his lap, and though he was staring straight ahead like a giant toad, I knew he was watching everything. He was one of Crane's men. He had that look.

"I already asked about him," Jeremy whispered. "He's delivering something to Singapore. Freaky guy, huh?"

I looked back at him, but now his eyes were focused right on me. I quickly ducked and hid behind my giant seat.

Once we were in the air, I never really relaxed, even though traveling on a private jet was amazing. Susan brought us deli-cious breakfast items — chocolate-covered waffles, omelets, crispy bacon, pancakes, pastries, fresh-squeezed orange juice.

Twenty hours is a lot of time to kill. Trevor and I watched movies, played video games, talked — while all throughout Susan kept bringing us more delicious food, comfy blan-kets, sleep blindfolds, anything we wanted before we even knew we wanted it.

When Trevor fell asleep, I paced the aisle with my tape recorder, recording the engines and other plane sounds. I was careful to stay as far away as I could from the bag with the dolphin helmet. The last thing I wanted was to touch it and have that painful sound penetrate my mind again. Just flying on an airplane was terrifying enough. The thought of combining that fear with the awful sound-bending experi-ence the helmet put me through was totally unbearable.

Sound bending. How quickly I had come to accept the fact that, for better or for worse, I had this amazing power. Yet how little I understood it. I knew that on the island I would need my power to be at its strongest, but I still hardly understood how or why it worked. I had no control over it. Why did it work sometimes and not others? How could I get it to be a part of me, and not just some strange floating current that possessed me whenever it wanted?

I was tired but I was afraid to let myself fall asleep. Eventually, my body won the battle with my mind, and I drifted off.

It wasn't a peaceful sleep, though. Bad dreams filled with scary images and sounds wouldn't let me rest. The horrible humanlike wail from the purple swirl of light was everywhere, though sometimes morphing into the eerie wail of the theremin. I was on a submarine, barreling through icebergs, with a desperate mission. The toadlike guy was there, too. But he was a double agent and he wouldn't listen to me. Then I was in a plane, skimming along the water like a bird of prey. It was terrifying. We were losing control. The water was violent with waves and whirlpools. We were flying dangerously low, everything was shaking. The plane . . . it was crashing!

"Mom!" I screamed. I felt soft hands on my shoulders tuck the blanket securely around me.

"It's okay, Leo. Only a little turbulence. We're on the descent, and we'll land within thirty minutes."

"I'm okay," I said, slowly coming to the realization that it was Susan and not my mom. I looked around the edge of my chair for the toad guy. He was gone.

The descent was bumpy. Jiggling all around and dropping like a roller coaster. Everything was rattling. I listened for any sign of engine malfunction, but I couldn't hear any —

not that I would have known what it sounded like anyway. Susan was nowhere to be seen. I glanced over at Jeremy, and he was hunched over, holding a barf bag in his hands. The plane made a sudden drop, and I heard the sound of falling plates from the kitchen.

I looked out the window and the sky was gray and misty. I couldn't see the horizon, just the blinking red light on the wing that was writhing in the turbulent air. I thought maybe I was going to barf, too. Just then, the clouds melted away and brilliant golden yellow rays of the sun streaked through the window and lit up the blue sky so that it was almost glowing. It was the most beautiful thing I had ever seen, and I was so happy that I watched that transformation take place right in front of my eyes. Immediately the plane stabilized. Down below was pure turquoise water.

"Everything's okay," I said to Jeremy, who was still hunched over. I reached behind my seat and patted him on the arm.

"Dry land," Jeremy moaned. "I'm going to kiss the runway."

We flew closer and closer to the water until I could see the crests of the turquoise waves. I saw the outline of the island, sandy beaches on its edge, green jungle in the interior. There was one road running around the island, and only a few buildings.

We touched down on a bumpy little runway and taxied to a stop.

While Susan opened the door, Trevor and I gathered up our gear and made our way down the aisle. I glanced back to see if Crane's man had reappeared. There he was, cleaning his fingernails with a huge pocketknife. I noticed that he was missing the top of his index finger. Strange how everyone who worked for Crane seemed to be missing some hunk of their body.

The staff and crew of the plane gathered in a straight line by the exit, looking fresh and crisp in their perfect outfits.

"Have fun, boys," Susan said as she rubbed our arms.

Outside, the island air was warm but with a soft breeze. As we stepped onto the tiny landing strip, I realized that both Trevor and I had put on our parkas and beanies, as if we were still in New York.

"Guys," Jeremy called from behind us, "New York is six thousand miles that way. We're in the tropics, show some skin!"

A bright yellow jeep came hurtling along a dirt road toward us, sending clouds of dust into the air. It came to a sharp stop right in the middle of the landing strip. A young woman hopped over the door, dusted herself off, then waved her hands and yelled, "Welcome! Hi! Hi!" I could see that she was really tall and wearing only jean shorts, flip-flops, and a golden bikini top. Everything about her glowed that same golden tan color.

"Well, hello right back at ya," I heard Jeremy whisper under his breath.

"Welcome to Palmira," she said when she reached us. "I'm Dr. Rebecca Cabot, chief of marine biology here at the reserve. But you can call me Becky. We're pretty informal here."

Even her eyes were that same golden color. She was solid and rugged, and her strong-looking feet had almost molded into her wafer-thin flip-flops.

"Hi, Becky," Trevor and I managed to stammer. She was beautiful.

"What's your name?" she asked, shaking Trevor's hand.

"Trevor," he mumbled. He was embarrassed and thrilled at the same time.

"Trevor! What a great name. I bet you're a budding science genius, with such focused eyes."

"Uh — I . . . try to —"

"I knew it! And what's your name?" she said, scooting toward me.

"He's Leo Lomax," Jeremy said. "And I'm his tutor, Jeremy Sebold. I happen to almost hold a PhD myself."

"Really? In what subject?"

"Ethnomusicology," he said. "With a specialty in independent North Carolina funk recordings from 1964 to 1972."

"Oh, I didn't know they gave advanced degrees in that," Becky said. "We're not quite so hip in the biological sciences."

Up close like this, I noticed how tall she was. In another life, with those shoulders, she could have been a champion beach volleyball player. She was wearing a small sand dollar on a piece of string around her neck. And she had a dolphin tattoo above her waist.

"Come on, gentlemen," she said. "We've got a beautiful drive to the reserve. I'll tell you all about the flora and fauna as we drive. I'm like a human field guide. Just yawn if I get boring."

"Why do I think none of us will be yawning?" Jeremy said with a smile.

Wait a minute. Was Jeremy flirting with her? I had never seen him flirt, never even considered the possibility that he knew how.

"I want to hear everything," Trevor said, his voice cracking. "I'm very fascinated by . . . um . . . women of science."

I just stared at Trevor. Call me crazy, but I swear he was flirting, too. Was I the only sane person there? We were here to learn, to solve a scientific mystery, to find answers, not to act like idiots in front of Dr. Cabot. Besides, Trevor was thirteen and she must have been thirty. Oh well, I guess a guy can dream.

Becky seemed unaware of all the attention she was getting. She ran off toward the convertible jeep and hopped into the driver's seat.

"Shotgun!" Jeremy and Trevor both called in unison, racing each other to see who could sit next to her first. Again, Becky ignored them.

"Come on, Leo," she said, patting the seat next to her. "I'm saving this for you. Dr. Lylo tells me your father was a very brilliant man. I want to hear all about him."

She waited for us to climb in and we took off along the bumpy road that hugged the shore. I wasn't sure where we were going or what we would find, but if the rest of Palmira was anything like Becky, I knew it was going to be good.

CHAPTER 21

We drove along a rough dirt road, thicketed by deep green bushes and trees. Some of the islanders were walking by the side of the road, carrying bundles of green branches on their backs. Becky waved at each passing person and they all waved back warmly. When we passed a hilly area covered in low bushes with little white flowers, she said, "That's *Ageratum conyzoides L.*"

The Latin words rolled out of her mouth like she said them every day.

"I knew that," Jeremy joked. "Doesn't everybody?"

"Bet you didn't know it's also known as goat weed," she said, revving the engine to get up the hill.

"Goat weed!" Trevor said. "I read an article in *Scientific American* about how it's used for medicinal purposes, like to cure diarrhea and intestinal worms."

Clueless as I am about women, even I knew that for a guy with a big crush, talking about diarrhea and stomach worms is not the right move to impress someone. But I was wrong. Becky was the exception.

"It's good for vomiting, too," she said enthusiastically. "I read that same issue, Trevor. Did you get to the article about acoustic pollution and marine mammals? It explains how military sonar can ruin the hearing of beaked whales and dolphins. In fact, whale recordings from the nineteen sixties and nineteen seventies sound much different than they do now. Those were happier, quieter times."

"I didn't get a chance to finish the issue," Trevor said. "Leo and I got busy doing some sound experiments of our own."

"I'd like to hear about them."

"Great, let's make a date and we'll talk science."

"I'd like that, Trevor."

He was really pleased with himself. He shot me a thumbs-up but Jeremy just looked at him and said, "Get real, my man."

"So is that what brings you here, Leo?" Becky asked me. "Your sound experiments?"

"Yes. I need to learn about dolphin sounds — as fast as I can. One in particular."

"You sound like a man in a hurry."

"I am. I need to talk with Dr. Lylo about some recordings my dad was a part of. The dolphin sounds on them are totally freaky. The ones that almost sound human, but aren't."

"Those were made back in the day, Leo. The dolphins actually made a few of those sounds on their own, and Jay — Dr. Lylo — thought they were mimicking human speech, or maybe trying to communicate. So he trained a group of dolphins to make those sounds, hoping it would be the foundation for interspecies communication. It was quite an insight."

"Why?" I asked.

"Because he believed that dolphin intelligence is based on highly developed emotional states, states we don't have words for, states that more closely resemble music than anything else. So he trained them to make sounds we could hear with our own ears, that we could react to — but that was back when Jay was still conducting those types of experiments on dolphins."

"What kind of experiments is he currently running?" Trevor asked, sounding about thirty years older than thirteen.

"We don't experiment," Becky answered in a low, serious voice. "Not in the traditional sense. Not anymore. Now we just observe and experience."

"But that's not very scientific," Trevor said. "How can you get any verifiable results?"

"There's a lot you can learn just by observing the dolphins, Trevor. And the scientific journals have forgotten that another path to knowledge is *experience*. Personal experience. Dolphins are amazing, beautiful beings. I love working with them. There's nothing in the world that's better than throwing yourself into the things you love."

"That's how I felt when I discovered real music," Jeremy said. "I grew up in the sticks with nothing but country and bubblegum pop. Then one day I heard the godfather of soul, James Brown, on vinyl, and I was a goner. I wouldn't sell that record for a million dollars."

Becky gave Jeremy a really deluxe smile.

"I admire your passion," she said. If it had been a movie, I swear they would have kissed right then and there. But it wasn't a movie, and Jeremy was in the backseat anyway, and besides, I hadn't flown all this way to watch a smooch fest.

"Are we almost there?" I asked Becky.

"Another couple miles, Leo. You're so impatient!"

I couldn't wait to get there. I had so many questions to ask.

"Why did Lylo stop the experiments?" I asked.

"He felt it was wrong to lock up social, intelligent creatures in little solitary pens. Dolphins have been around for thirty million years, with brains bigger than our own. Over the years he'd gotten to know them very closely, and saw them suffering. Some even lost the will to live, and stopped breathing until they drowned."

"Dolphin suicide?" Trevor asked.

"As scientists, we try not to anthropomorphize . . . er . . . attach human concepts to nonhuman animals. But in this line of work, that's difficult to do. You'll see. Jay called it the 'weirdness factor.' And when he saw his dolphins deciding not to breathe anymore, he stopped the experiments. They were like brothers and sisters to him—you wouldn't be cruel to your brother, would you, Leo?"

Why did she have to bring that up? I was already feeling horrible that I was here in the South Pacific having left Hollis back in New York, with no brother to watch his show.

Up ahead, the dirt road was coming to a dead end at a cluster of buildings and cabins strung out along the shore. We came to a stop and I got out of the car and looked around. About six or seven white buildings were grouped together along a path made of crushed seashells. A path running alongside them splintered off in two directions, one way leading to some high cliffs and the other path leading to a rocky beach surrounding a lagoon. A wooden sign at the entrance to the main bungalow read: FRIENDSHIP COVE — CENTER FOR HUMAN/DOLPHIN RELATIONS.

As we got our stuff out of the jeep, I made sure that Trevor grabbed the duffel with the dolphin helmet. I was already dreading showing that horrible contraption to Jay Lylo. Here he was, amidst all these people devoting their lives to protect the dolphins. And here I was, carrying a big chunk of evil into paradise.

"Would you like me to show you around the reserve?" Becky asked.

"Actually, I'd like to meet Dr. Lylo as soon as possible," I answered.

"You can show me around," Jeremy said. "We'll drop the guys off at Lylo's and you can give me the deluxe tour."

"The property's big and it's a bit of a hike," Becky said. "You'll need sun protection."

She leaned into the back of the jeep and pulled out some

baseball caps. She handed one to Jeremy, then plopped one on Trevor's head and one on mine. As I reached up to adjust it, I suddenly felt a flash of current, then heard the velvety voice of Gary Cohen, legendary announcer for the New York Mets.

"Alex Rodriguez digs in as R. A. Dickey checks for the sign. Dickey deals. Knuckleball. A-Rod connects. Long fly ball to left field. Jason Bay gives chase, back, back, back to the wall . . . It's outta there! A three-run home run. That'll pretty much close the book on today's effort, right, Keith?"

I heard a roomful of men groan and murmur angrily.

"They don't let just anyone wear the pinstripes, boys," one obnoxious guy taunted. "You gotta be a true Yankee!"

"Joey, I'm gonna make you eat that hat."

"Just try it."

I put my hands on my ears to drown out the reverberating sound of a crosstown rivalry about to get physical. Trevor saw me and knew that I was sound bending.

"Leezer? You okay?"

I saw his lips moving, but I couldn't hear his voice, just the sound of the crowd on the TV. He reached over and pulled the cap off my head. Immediately the noise ceased, and I was back on the island, listening to the palm fronds rustling in the afternoon breeze.

I looked at the hat in his hand. It was a Yankees hat, all right, and I knew somebody had watched Alex Rodriguez smack a dinger. Becky was looking at me curiously.

"Obviously, Leo, you don't like the hat."

"Thanks, Becky, but the Yankees make me sick. I'm a Mets fan all the way."

"Understood," she said. "I'm always an underdog fan myself."

We started up the seashell path that led to the cliffs. Jeremy and Becky walked ahead of us, talking and laughing.

"Tough break, Trev," I said as we followed behind them. "Looks like Jeremy's getting the upper hand here."

"The day's not over yet, Leezer. One way or the other, I'll get her to notice me."

Trevor was so intent on what he was saying that he tripped over a wooden caution sign and went stumbling to his knees trying desperately not to do a total face plant on the seashell path.

"I'm fine," he said, as Becky came running to help him up. Brushing the bits and pieces of shells off his elbows, he whispered, "That wasn't quite what I had in mind."

We hiked all the way up to the high cliff overlooking the cove, passing a tented area called the Pod where the scientists and caretakers hung out. Becky told us there were twenty-three people living on the reserve, taking care of thirty-one dolphins. We passed the rehabilitation tanks where dolphins were kept when they were being treated by the vet. Beyond the tanks were the research wing and library.

"We have books, movies, recordings, articles — anything on the record about dolphins," Becky called to me. "Whatever you need for your research."

Just before we left the rehabilitation tank area, I thought I heard music, playing far away and strangely muffled.

"Does anyone hear that?" I asked. "That weird music?"

"Yeah, Leo, that's from Jabari's tank," Becky said. "He loves music."

"Really?" I saw Jabari in his tank, just floating around and twirling in slow motion, like those guys who do tai chi down in Chinatown.

"He has a cord he can pull whenever he wants to listen to music. He listens *all day long*. He likes classical music, really slow string pieces. The violin is his favorite."

I listened closer. I wondered if there were any recordings of my mom on that playlist.

"Why only classical?" Jeremy sighed. "Why don't you pump in some Curtis, or Mingus, or even Fahey?"

"I don't have the faintest idea who you're talking about." Becky laughed. "We play him classical because that's the music we know about. But maybe, while you're here, you could see if we can spice up his listening."

"Make a dolphin mixtape?" Jeremy's eyes popped out. "Man, definitely, I've already got volumes one through seven planned in my head."

We continued along the trail until we got to a clearing. I hadn't realized we had walked that far uphill, but we were standing on the top of a 300-foot sheer cliff of black rocks that looked out onto the pure blue ocean. Down below, the waves were crashing into the rock walls and the wind swept the spray all the way up to us. I walked out to the ledge until all I could see was the ocean. It was thrilling and terrifying at the same time. I wanted to extend my arms like a giant bird. Trevor joined me at the cliff's edge.

"How much better is this than the East River?" he asked me.

"I wish I could relax and enjoy it," I said. "But all I can think about is . . . "

"I know, Leezer. The dolphin helmet. It's not like you haven't mentioned it before."

"Look, Trev, I don't mean to be such a pain, but this stuff is all I can think about. My power. What it means. That sound. Why it haunts me so much I'm afraid to close my eyes. And there's no one with answers. No one to calm me down but me."

We stood there silently for a moment, looking out at the view. I could tell Trevor was trying to think of something comforting to say. But when you got right down to it, what I had spoken was the truth and we both knew it.

The cliff looked out over a giant cove that seemed to be almost scooped out of the island. The water was a lighter shade of turquoise there, dotted with reefs and sand bars.

"We're heading to the protected cove," Becky said as we hiked down the steep trail that led down to the beach. "That's where we do most of our observing. We're trying every way we can think of to communicate with the dolphins. The whole lagoon is rigged with different mics and cameras, we've got computer science people trying to establish a dolphin dictionary, we even employ researchers who just play with the dolphins like kids. The dolphins don't venture out in open water. They know they wouldn't make it."

"Why not?" I asked.

"Because, Leo, they were all captive dolphins. All they know are tanks and doing tricks to get a fish. Jump through this hoop, jump through that one. They don't have sufficient survival skills to live in the ocean."

We passed a dock with a few rowboats, and at the far end, it led to a small two-story house.

"That's the Dolphin House," Becky said, pointing to the house at the end of the beach. "Jay's supposed to meet you there."

Becky explained before we even had a chance to ask.

"Jay had this idea to build a house that was partially flooded with water, so the dolphins could swim in and interact with us like a family. We finally got it built last year."

She pushed open the front door of the house, which led to the top floor. "Knock, knock. Anyone home?"

I'd never seen anything quite like the Dolphin House. Its top floor looked like a regular place. There appeared to be a living room/office kind of combination with a couch and other stuff. But its bottom floor was sitting right in the water, submerged almost.

As she looked around for Lylo, my heart started to race. I had the same kind of feeling that I'd had before I played the blue disc. That I was about to learn about a part of myself I never knew existed.

"He should be along any minute," Becky said. "You guys okay to wait here by yourselves?"

We nodded and she and Jeremy left. Trevor watched them go.

"You do realize that this gives him a tremendous advantage, don't you?" he said to me.

"I need you here, Trev. I'm pretty nervous."

Trevor shook his head. "The things I do for friendship. One day you'll thank me."

"How about today?" I said, giving him a big and awkward slap on the back. It was another one of those "I love you, man" moments.

We went downstairs. It smelled damp and fishy down there, like the touch pool at the New York Aquarium. The floors were made of the same polished wood as upstairs, but after a few feet, the floor dropped off and the other half of the room was water. Two hammocks were strung across the room, hanging about three feet over the water. The far side of the room was completely open and looked out onto the whole blue cove.

"Okay, this is officially too strange for me. Weirdness factor times infinity," Trevor said. "I'm going back upstairs. I'm fried. I might just pass out on the couch for a few."

Trevor tossed the duffel onto a blue chair that looked like it was made of rubber, then headed upstairs.

Suddenly, I felt overwhelmingly tired and those hammocks looked really comfortable. I grabbed the netting of one of them and leapt in, which was no easy task. Once I was in it, the thing swung back and forth like crazy, but as I settled in, it rocked slower and slower.

I laid my hands behind my head, and looked out at the turquoise lagoon. I wondered what Lylo would be like. Would he tell me what that terrible sound was, and why it filled me with fear? Would he make me feel safe, like my dad did? Or would he leave me with more questions than answers? I let my arm hang over the side of the hammock, dangling it in the water below. A piece of purple kelp floated by, and twisted itself around my fingers, bringing with it that familiar sound-bending feeling, followed by a medley of sounds. I heard the call of whales. The jabber of dolphins. A rusty anchor chain being reeled in. The leafy, watery rustle of a kelp forest. The bark of a sea otter. It was an entire ecosystem, swimming in my head.

I closed my eyes and fell asleep, the sound of underwater life alive in my ears.

CHAPTER 22

When I woke up, I knew time had passed, but I had no idea how long. It took a minute to remember where I was. I was so comfortable in that hammock, rocking back and forth and gazing through half-open eyes at the wood beams high up in the ceiling. I heard a creaking sound, like an old door being swung open and shut on rusty hinges. It was really close by. Suddenly, something slapped the water beneath me, making a sound like metal hitting metal. I felt some spray on my face. And a being right near me.

I rolled over on my side toward the open ocean and two feet from my head I saw another head—a large gray head, with black eyes, and a big open beak with rows of teeth and a long mouth that was almost smiling. A dolphin!

I was wide-awake now, my heart pulsing and my breath coming fast. Tingles ran up and down my body. The dolphin rolled over, showing me its white belly, then flipped back over, smacked its tail against the water, and opened its mouth up to me, with that creaking sound coming out of it. Its blowhole was opening and closing shut. Did it want to play? What should I do?

With a splash, the dolphin rose higher out of the water, clicking at me. To my amazement, it rested its head right on the hammock, and opened its mouth wide, just inches from me. I twitched with panic, felt my body lurch with such force that the hammock flipped completely over and sent me splashing into the water.

I closed my eyes in fear. I heard lots of little rustlings of the water. My arms and legs flailed until my hand touched the slippery skin of the dolphin. Underwater I heard its high-pitched squeaks and whistles. I opened my eyes and the dark, blurry shape of its head was right in front of my face. For a moment, I felt like we almost recognized each other. Then it was gone and I felt it underneath me, pushing me to the surface. I gasped the fresh air as it pushed me toward the wooden ledge.

The commotion had awakened Trevor, who flew down the stairs to my rescue.

"What happened?" he shouted as I shook my head, my whole body electric, with a huge smile on my face.

"Whoa!" was all I could say. I heard more of the creaking sound, and although I couldn't believe it, the dolphin was still by the ledge with its long mouth open, showing us its teeth and, I swear, smiling at us.

"Freddy is such a ham," a new voice said. I couldn't pinpoint where the voice was coming from until my eye caught a glimpse of a human head in the water. He had a pointy gray beard, a full head of gray hair, and a goofy smile. "Freddy still loves the spotlight, don't you, Freddy?" he said. "He wants you to rub his tongue."

"What?" I said.

"Yeah, they love it," the man said. "He won't bite, go ahead."

I kneeled down and rubbed the dolphin's huge pink tongue. It was pretty rough and a little gross, but I could tell Freddy loved it because he made more clicking sounds, then flipped over on his back and showed me his white underside. I rubbed that, too. I wanted to take Freddy home with me.

Meanwhile, the man in the water had pulled himself up onto the wooden floor and was standing on the other side of the room, his small blue bathing suit dripping seawater.

"Freddy just wants to meet his new houseguests," he said. I recognized his voice from the dolphin record. It was Jay Lylo.

"Here, try it, Trev, he's gentle," I said. Trevor nervously bent down over the dolphin, extended one finger and rubbed it on Freddy's tongue. Freddy made more clicks and squeaks.

I started to introduce myself to Lylo, but that wasn't necessary.

"Leo, you look just like your father." He pawed at his ear, shaking some of the seawater out. "Same cheeks, too!" Then he squeezed one of my cheeks with his wet hand, though unlike when Crane did it, I didn't mind. "You're like a little version of Kirk."

"You and my dad were friends, right?"

"Friends in thinking," he answered, "which is the best kind of friend. I was so sorry to hear about his passing. He was a great man."

"That's okay," I said. "Thanks so much for letting us stay here. That's my best friend, Trevor. The smartest guy I know."

"Trevor, an honor and a privilege."

"I like Freddy," was all that Trevor could get out. He was still running that same finger on his tongue.

Lylo grabbed a towel off a nearby hook and began to dry himself off. I was hoping he might cover up a bit after he was dry, but he didn't. He was very unusual looking. He had these bright blue slitty eyes, and a kind of beaklike mouth that was plastered into a wild smile. He almost looked like a dolphin.

"How'd you meet my dad?" I asked him.

"Let's see. Kirk, how did I meet Kirk? Well, way back before you were born, CDs used to come on these black—"

"Records," I said with a smile.

He slapped his head. "How silly of me, you're Kirk's son. Of course, you know about records. I actually made one a long time ago, your dad introduced me to the people at Folkways—"

"You mean, *Sounds and Ultra-Sounds of the Bottle-Nose Dolphin?*"

"Leo, you're blowing my mind here. How did you—"

"I heard it in my friend's record store. That's actually what brought us here."

"Leo, my man, I don't know why you're here, but I think we're gonna be pals." Then he squeezed my cheek again. "You're perfect!"

I liked Dr. Lylo a lot. I understood why he and my dad were friends. Though he was pretty old, he had the bounce of a kid, just the way he looked at everything, and his huge, goofy smile. I glanced back over at my bag on the blue rubber chair. I wondered how perfect I'd be once I told Jay what was inside. I had to tell him about that contraption right away, no more secrets, no time to waste. I took a deep breath and opened my mouth. Just then, I heard a splash. Another dolphin was in the house, twirling and squeaking and clicking.

"Ah, Tami's here, too!" Jay cried. "Why don't you hop in with them, Trevor? You and Freddy seem to be buddies."

"Thanks, Dr. Lylo, but I'm comfortable right here."

"Doctor? Doctor! Jay, please. Please! I'm going to shower off real quick. You guys keep Tami and Freddy company." And before I had a chance, Jay had bounced out of sight.

I don't know what came over me, but before I knew it, I had snuck up behind Trevor and pushed him into the water with my knee. At first, he screamed in fright, but then a second later, his head popped up and he was laughing as hard as I'd ever heard him laugh. I jumped right in after him.

Tami and Freddy clicked and squeaked and swirled around us. Twirling, darting, spinning. So free and full of joy. Trevor and I were becoming friends with them; it was just like playing with a couple of new kids at the public

pool. Making up games, laughing, splashing — all of us connected and just enjoying being together in the water. Every
now and then I'd feel these weird zaps of energy, electric
pulses that ran up and down my spine and gave me a pure
rush. The dolphins moved just like those purple whirlpools
of light in my vision. But then I felt that creeping darkness
again, and I thought I heard a beeping. Pulling away from
the group, I remembered that device in my bag. My chest
tightened. I felt like I was suffocating. I heaved myself out of
the water and flopped on the wood like a beached whale.

As I rubbed the water from my eyes, I noticed that the
duffel bag was lying open on the floor, unzipped. Sitting on
the blue chair was Jay, and in his hands was the device.

CHAPTER 23

Jay was slumped over, slowly turning the device around in his fingertips. Even though he was still only wearing those tiny blue trunks, he looked like a different person. His puffy cheeks had flattened and his eyes were almost closed shut. He looked weak and fragile, and suddenly seemed much older.

All I wanted to do was slither back into the water and forget all this, everything. Anything to get away from this terrible tightness in my chest. But I stood upright. Drops of water pattered onto the wood floor. Jay looked up.

"I didn't mean to pry, Leo. Something was beeping in the bag. Someone's phone. I just wanted to turn it . . . " He trailed off.

"No, Jay, I'm sorry."

"What on earth for? You didn't make the device." He dropped it on the chair and covered it up with the bag.

The entire room was quiet except for the softly lapping water. The dolphins must have swum away. I heard Trevor get out of the water and felt him at my side.

"That thing is the reason we're here," I said. "We knew it was something for a dolphin, and a terrible piece of electronics, but that was it." I wiped some water from my face.

"It's a helmet for a dolphin," he said quietly. "And it's military."

"Military?" I asked. "Whose military?"

"Does it really matter?" Jay sighed. "Ours, theirs, what's the difference? All those fools all over the world, churning out their weapons of destruction."

He stood up and paced angrily around the room, his blue eyes like lightning bolts. "History is riddled with them. Little men who want to play war. Little men who want a bigger gun than the other guy. Country after country, hell-bent on destroying it all. For what? Peace?" He laughed savagely. "No, just power-hungry people who want to take everything good in this world, everything sacred, and twist it into its opposite. *Twist a thirty-million-year-old intelligence into a weapon!*"

Jay flopped back into the chair and closed his eyes. Trevor and I were stunned, frozen. Not to mention soaking wet. Jay got up and handed us some towels.

"Where did you get this thing?" he asked.

"We stole it from my uncle," I said.

"Your uncle?"

"Yeah, my stepuncle Crane — the guy who's taking care of my brother and me. He buys and sells rare artifacts."

"Artifacts?" Jay laughed. "Well, I suppose it is an artifact. But you guys did the right thing. Nobody should make money off of this."

"Jay," Trevor cut in, "have you seen this before?"

"Not specifically, Trevor. But I have an idea where it came from. When I first started my research on dolphins, all these military types were trying to butt their way into my work. I thought their interest was just about submarines and sonar, until I heard later that they were training dolphins, using them as soldiers. Using them to detect underground mines with their echolocation."

I thought of Freddy and Tami, so carefree and playful. I couldn't see them as soldiers, not in a million years.

"When America found out that the Russians were using dolphins, then we had to have better-trained, better-equipped dolphins than they did. And then they had to outdo us! It was called the Cold War. I've even heard that countries strapped bombs onto them and sent them on suicide missions."

He paused, unable to go on. I stared at that helmet in disgust. No wonder it had sent out such strong vibrations to me.

"Is that a bomb, Jay?" I asked, stepping away from it.

"No, Leo. But it is one more reason why we don't deserve this planet of ours."

"It doesn't have to be like that," I said. "We can figure out what this does, and let everybody know the way that dolphins have been used. If people know the truth, they won't let it happen again."

"Maybe we can start by you telling us what the helmet does," Trevor said, pulling out his spiral notebook and mechanical pencil.

Jay uncovered the helmet and held it weakly in his hands.

"I don't know," he said. "From the look of it, it transfers energy."

"That's what I thought," Trevor said. "But from what?"

"From the dolphin," Jay said morosely. "These needles . . ." And he sighed loudly. ". . . they probably went straight into the inner ear and imaging region of its brain. The echolocation centers."

"And who would have had the technology to make something like this?" Trevor asked, taking notes like crazy.

"They were built many years ago. Had to be either the Americans or the Russians."

When I heard him mention the Russians again, all I could think of was those guys who had been visiting Crane. The Russian men in fancy suits who had visited the fourth floor of the warehouse. Those same Russian men who were supposed to be receiving crate number 11910091005122622. The crate with the helmet. Everything clicked into place. No doubt, they were buying the helmet to hide it, so the world wouldn't know what they had created.

How could he? I thought. How could Crane make a fortune off a twisted, sick, awful device like that helmet?

Trevor stood up abruptly.

"Okay, I think I've got enough," he said.

"Enough for what?" I asked.

"I'm going to the library. There's got to be something there, some evidence of how these were used, and when. If it's there, I'll find it. The first step to fixing a problem is knowledge."

He looked at the device hard for a moment, threw off his towel, and flew from the room, wet sneakers squeaking and squishing on the wood.

"Trevor has a bright future ahead of him," Jay said.

"Yeah, he's the smartest guy I know. He has five of the hardest unsolved physics problems pinned above his desk."

"Ah, the promise of youth! Sorry for the fireworks there, Leo. I've spent years trying to build this reserve with love. And seeing that helmet, well, it made me think that all my work here has been for nothing. But now when I see you kids coming out here, on your own, well . . . what do you say we get some fresh air?"

Before I could answer, Jay was running up the stairs, two at a time. I followed him outside into the warm, clear air. As we started down the path, we met a red-haired guy with a bright red beard, carrying a notebook filled with papers.

"Leo! This is one of my postgrad students, Sasha Olevski. He's visiting from the Moscow University. Sasha is developing a way to actually take three-dimensional *pictures* of dolphin vocalizations and echolocations."

"Wow," I said. I wished Trevor had been there to translate.

Jay gave Sasha a warm slap on the back, then he and I continued up the hill. As we rose higher up on the rocky path, I looked over the whole lagoon and saw all the different scientists in rowboats on the sparkling blue water and heard the echoes of dolphin squeaks and clicks. The sun was an hour from setting so the whole lagoon was almost glowing a brilliant orange. It felt good here. I didn't ever want to go back to Brooklyn and Crane's cold, unhappy warehouse.

"Maybe this is where I should be," I thought aloud.

"Leo, Leo, not yet," Jay answered. "Something tells me you've got a lot more work to do on planet Earth."

"Do you think you could tell me more about echolocation, Jay?" I asked.

"Everything I know, buddy."

"Because, um, I kind of have something similar," I blurted out. I hadn't meant to, but Jay seemed so wise. If there was anybody in the world who could help me understand my power and what I was supposed to do with it, he was the one. He looked at me with a half smile, as if he knew a joke nobody else did.

"Why am I not surprised, Leo? And don't think for a minute I don't know there's more to your story than you've let on. You come here out of the blue, after hearing my record, bringing with you this . . . Suppose you start at the beginning."

Jay seemed to know my feelings before I even did. Did he have a special power, too? My head was racing: What should I tell him? What should I tell him first? Would it make sense? Would he laugh? Just as I opened my mouth, I heard someone screaming my name. It was Jeremy. He was on top of the hill, holding his cell phone and nervously tugging on his beard. From the pit I felt in my stomach, I already knew: He'd been Craned.

"Leo, what have you done?" Jeremy demanded, as he ran up to me, waving his cell phone like it was on fire. "I'm going to be in such deep—what did you do?"

"Nothing!"

"Leo, Crane's left me about a dozen messages. I've never heard someone that mad before. He says you stole something from him."

"It wasn't his in the first place," I said firmly.

"Hey, I'm on your side. I don't know what you did, but Crane is a raving maniac. He's coming for you."

"Here?"

"In the flesh. Getting on a plane and chasing you down. He said he's taking off in fifteen minutes. And that was a half hour ago."

Crane. There was no escaping him. As we watched the sun set over the lagoon, I felt like the sun was setting on my mission, too. Crane would be here in twenty hours, maybe less. It was all for nothing. I'd be grounded for life, and so would Trevor, and if there were a way for Crane to ground Jeremy, he'd find it. I'd have to live with the pain of that little purple swirl in my head forever, and the constant fear of hearing it in my nightmares. How long would it stay with me? Until it was dead? Was it dead already? All I knew was that I failed it. Some rite of passage.

"*Glubokaya Zamorozka*," I heard from behind me.

"Huh?" I said as I spun around, half expecting to find Dmitri or Klevko. It was Trevor, panting hard from running up the hill, holding his notebook with his mechanical pencil clipped to the front. He must have met Becky at the library, because she was right behind him.

"Project Glubokaya Zamorozka, that's Russian for *deep freeze*," Trevor said.

"Tell them, Trevor!" Becky wasn't out of breath in the least. "Leo, what a mind your friend has! I've never seen such focus in my entire life." Becky patted his shoulder as Trevor grinned at Jeremy.

Trevor cleared his throat and stood up straight.

"So the helmet was part of this top secret Russian experiment that ran from the nineteen seventies until it was cancelled in the mid nineteen eighties. The idea was to create a roving anti-sonar device that would jam US submarines — with the dolphin wearing this helmet."

"What happened to the dolphins after the project ended?" I asked, clinging to a childish hope that there would be a happy ending to this story.

"It didn't say. And as far as I could tell, the project was only operational once. On a small island in the South Pacific. It was called Makuna."

"Makuna?" Jay blurted out. "Makuna is only fifty miles from here."

"No way!" I cried. "Maybe there are some dolphins still there, maybe some are alive. That's possible, isn't it, Jay?"

"Very unlikely, Leo."

"But we can find out for ourselves, right?" I said. "Can we go?"

"We're not even sure what we're looking for," Jay said. "What are you expecting to find, Leo?"

"I don't know, or at least, I can't say it in words. But I know this, Jay. So many strange things have led me to right here and everything in my body is telling me that I have to go to that island. That I have to follow this helmet and see where it takes me."

I didn't tell him about my vision of the purple swirl calling out for help. Or how the helmet was leading me to it, to him, to whatever it was. Instead, what I said was, "I feel like if we go there, we will save a life."

Jay nodded, studying my face with a long, thoughtful expression. At last he spoke. "I don't know how any person could say no to that."

Jeremy immediately started doing the calculations.

"Let's see. Crane is coming in twenty hours. How fast does your boat go?"

"Twelve knots per hour," Becky said.

"Which means if we leave in an hour," Jay said, "we have . . . let's see . . . carry the two . . . "

He looked at Jay and Becky for help. They just shrugged.

Trevor sighed loudly. "Seriously? Three PhDs and no one can do pre-algebra? Not even pre-algebra!"

"I'm not *exactly* a PhD, yet," Jeremy said, as Becky rolled her eyes at him.

"Really, it's such a trivial calculation. All you soft-science types should get over your fear of math —"

"Trevor! Can we make it?" I interrupted. I realized that Trevor was alone a lot of the time with his brilliant brain.

"Yeah, Leo. Assuming we leave in *two* hours — a more realistic time frame — and adding some extra travel time both ways, we should have about five hours once we get to the island."

"Then let's save a life!" I shouted. I felt that the voice was still alive. Already, I could feel its cry changing inside me. I heard hope in it now.

"Save a life! I love it!" Jay said, throwing his arms in the air. "Trevor, I could kiss that brain of yours." And then he reached out his hands, grabbed Trevor's head, and planted a huge kiss on his forehead. Trevor smiled awkwardly, then eyed Becky, probably hoping she'd plant one on him, too, but she just grinned and laughed. He'd have to settle for the old guy today.

"We leave in two hours," Jay said. "No time to waste."

I couldn't believe that my newly found power had brought me to this moment.

CHAPTER 24

t was already dark when we met down at the water, where the rowboats were waiting to take us out to the sailboat. The team consisted of Lylo, Becky, Trevor, me, and a guy named Cal from New Zealand who was an expert sailor. Jeremy was staying on the island to head off Crane. I had the helmet in my duffel bag—in case I needed to channel it again for clues.

There was an eerie mood on the lagoon as Becky rowed us out. I listened for the dolphins, but I couldn't hear them. A heavy fog hung on the water. When we saw the sailboat, she appeared from the mist like a ghost ship, her mast poking through the murk in the distance. She was called the *Flipper*. Whether that was in honor of the old TV show about the dolphin, or because the boat capsized a lot, I never learned.

We got on the *Flipper*. It was spotlessly clean with a huge mast, a real-deal wooden steering wheel, and a belowdecks cabin. Immediately, Jay began zipping around the boat in his bare feet, picking up ropes and putting them down, tightening things, tying knots, sailing stuff. I was pretty lost. Trevor tagged after Becky and tried to look like he knew what he was doing, even though I knew he had never set foot on a boat, not even in New York Harbor. Cal was busy pouring over a map and was writing figures down in a notebook, when not hollering at everybody.

"Can I have your attention?" Jay called out to us. "Cal tells me that this fog should dissipate once we get into open waters, and that if the weather holds and we keep a steady pace of ten knots, we should be there within five hours. We travel today to the abandoned island of Makuna, in the hopes of saving our brothers and sisters who were turned into instruments of war."

"Drop the anchors!" I cried, so moved by Jay's speech.

Everybody just stared at me. Trevor left Becky's side for a minute and sidled up to me.

"What we want to do, Leez, is hoist the anchor."

Cal gestured at us and barked more commands. After a few more minutes of preparation, Jay came by with a life jacket and gave it to me.

"Hey, Leo, want to try that again?"

"Hoist the anchors!" I cried.

"Raise the main sail at half-mast," Cal ordered. Jay leapt near the boom and tugged on a rope until a yellow sail was flapping in the light breeze. The boom swung out loosely to the left, the ship tilted slightly to the left and began to inch through the protected waters.

"You've launched a boat," Jay said to me with a sneaky grin.

Through the nighttime fog, I saw the charcoal outlines of the rock jetty. We were leaving the protected cove. The water was becoming a deeper shade of black as we sailed out into the open ocean. Except for the patter of feet on the deck and the flapping of the sail, it was almost silent.

"Raise the main sail," Cal cried, and the yellow sail shot up all the way to the top.

The boat picked up speed and seemed to shoot through the fog into a brilliant star-filled night. It was a tremendous feeling—we were now at the mercy of the currents and the wind, and for the first time, I truly felt the power of the ocean.

I looked back at the dark, foggy bowl of the lagoon. We were speeding away from it faster and faster.

Just then, a piercing whistle shot out through the fog. Trevor dashed to the back of the ship and called out, "See you soon, Freddy!" Jay and Becky both pursed their lips and made dolphin noises as loud as they could, and in return, a chorus of dolphin calls came back at us like a fun-house echo from the foggy confines of the cove.

Traveling on a sailboat was much different than I thought. Within thirty minutes, I was completely seasick. I couldn't help laughing to myself—for the past few days all I could think about was water and the ocean, and now that I was there, I was proving to be a very poor sailor.

"Leo, you're totally green, even in the starlight!" It was Becky.

"I'm gonna . . . " I just pointed meekly at the cabin.

"Don't go down there, sweetie. That'll really make you sick. There's a special spot for people without their sea legs, and it's the best view on the ship."

She pointed her long arm toward the bow, to a little spot that nosed out and was surrounded by all the protective wires that lined the whole ship.

"Just lay up there, Leo, and look straight ahead. You'll feel better!"

It took me a long time to creep up to the bow, but when I lay down with my head just edging ahead of the nose, I started to feel better. I inched myself farther out on the tip until all I saw was the dark sea ahead, and the starry skies above. The wind was whipping through my hair and a thin mist sprayed my face. It was like I was flying through space.

I looked down at the hull as it sliced through the water. We were gliding through the water so effortlessly — all I wanted to do was feel the ocean, let my hand turn into a rudder and trail through the warm waters. I reached down and let just the tips of my fingers skim the surface. It felt so good. I don't know why, but I felt like my parents were there with me. I felt that they were watching me, and that they were proud.

For a moment, I thought I heard my dad call my name, but when I turned, I realized it was just Jay joining me on the bow. He sat down, his feet dangling off the boat. I sighed.

"Expecting someone else?" he asked, but when he saw my face, he put his hand on my back. "Were they with you?"

"I miss them so much," I said just above a whisper. "It makes me feel crazy things."

"No, it's not crazy. You felt it—that was undeniable. What you were feeling was love, and love is as real a thing as this boat."

"I never even got to look for them," I said to Jay. "Somehow I thought that by coming here, I could find them. But that was crazy. They're lost for good." I looked out at the black sea and the twinkling stars.

"Nothing is ever lost for good, Leo. Things change—one thing passes into the other. Your parents are gone, but you have them inside of you, you have all your memories of them. As long as you love them, I think they're still alive."

Jay gazed out longingly at the stars and rested his chin in his hand. I noticed that he was wearing a gold wedding ring on his other hand that he clinked against the deck of the boat. I never saw his wife on the island. He must have lost someone, too.

"Then how come I still feel so alone?" I said after a while.

"You know, Leo, after I realized how wrong it was to experiment on dolphins, I decided to experiment on myself. I wanted to experience what it was like to be a dolphin in a small tank, so I built one. Just a metal container slightly bigger than a coffin filled with warm water. I found that if I made the water almost body temperature, and added some salt to it, I could float for hours—no sights, no sounds, no smells."

That sounded a lot like what I experienced when I listened to that blue disc of my naming ceremony on the island — the feeling of floating in darkness, listening to the tide.

"But something strange happens when you shut off all your senses, Leo. After you've been in there awhile, you start to hear things, see things, almost like being awake in a dream. And sometimes I'd leave the tank, and travel to other spaces. Spaces that I thought were more real than the real world. But when I returned back to Earth, I couldn't share what I experienced with anyone else. They couldn't understand. I was alone."

Jay was describing exactly what it was like for me when I was sound bending.

"I know the feeling," I said to him. "The same thing happens to me."

Jay laughed aloud, but not at me. In that laugh I knew he felt endless compassion for me.

"Leo, nothing you say surprises me anymore!" He pinched my cheek. "Perfect!"

We were racing across the pitch-black sea now, the wind in our sails, the balmy night air soft as a pillow. Jay breathed in deeply and continued his story.

"That experience was humbling, Leo, and when I came back to planet Earth for good, I looked at the dolphins in a new light. I stopped trying to make them talk to me, and started trying to understand them. That loneliness you feel, Leo, would make no sense to a dolphin. Dolphins have no boundaries, because there are no boundaries in water. They have a group mind. They rely on one another—they have to. When one gets injured, his pod buddies will gather under him to keep him afloat. They are not separate like the Homo sapiens—us."

Jay paused for a moment and listened to the water. He was a really deep thinker, and if I were in school trying to understand him, I would have been lost. But just lying out under the stars on this boat, and the way he talked—the rhythm of it—made my mind clear and relaxed, taking in everything like a sponge, but also mixing his thoughts with my own.

"Take a look at the sail, Leo."

I spun around and looked.

"We both see the yellow sail, right? The same one?"

"Yeah."

"But in truth, we see different things. I see it from my point of view, you see it from yours—and that keeps us apart. Not so with the dolphins. When they send out a sound beam, it ricochets off something and comes back to them, and they form that picture in their mind. But every dolphin in the pod can also hear that same sound if they want, and make that same image. Imagine, Leo, if other people could see the world just like you?"

I imagined. I thought about all the secret rooms in Crane's house, all the lies I had told, all the misunderstandings that had arisen because of my power. About the distance between Hollis and me, which was the one that hurt the most. I wanted to reach out with my mind and talk with Hollis, reach out across the globe, the way that device in crate 11910091005122622 had reached out to me.

"I wish we could share thoughts like the dolphins," I said, feeling a wave of sadness sweep over me. "I feel so alone."

Jay reached out and gave me a hug, not a shoulder-bump hug, but a real human hug, one you just wanted to melt into and stay in forever.

"We aren't alone, Leo, we have each other. And this feeling that you and I have right now, this is all we've got. It's as close as humans can come to the dolphins' world. And what is it, if not love?"

While we were talking, it was like we were the only two people in the universe. I hadn't even noticed that the moon was in the sky. It was a crescent moon low on the horizon that shot a faint silver beam onto the black water ahead. I felt Jay's warmth and compassion. I felt my father comforting me, telling me not to be afraid. And though he had told me in his letter not to tell my secret to anyone, I heard him in my mind, loud and clear, urging me to tell Jay.

"Jay," I began hesitantly, "I want to tell you something. And it's going to sound crazy."

"Leo, I spent a long time in an isolation tank — trust me, I've already heard every weird thing you could possibly think of."

Jay lay flat on his belly and reached his hand down into the dark water. I gathered my courage and told him everything. Spilled my guts. About the move to Crane's new apartment. The letter from my dad, the discovery of my strange birth, that blue disc with my ancestral name, the fainting spells, the space where I could hear with my secret ear, the strange sound-bending power I was discovering day by day.

I told him about finding that helmet and hearing the underwater landscape and finding his record amidst thousands of other records. As I spoke, he didn't seem shocked at all. But when I described the sad, almost human cry of that one swirling purple whirlpool of light, he yanked his hand out of the water and brought it to his face. He seemed to age twenty years right in front of me.

"Leo, can you make that sound for me?" he asked.

"I can't."

"Ever?"

"Well, sometimes when I'm sound bending, if it's a really strong sensation, Trevor says I make some sounds."

The moment he heard that, Jay hopped to his feet and grabbed me by my arm, leading me toward the cabin.

"Where are we going?" I said.

"To the helmet. I have to hear this for myself. I have to know if it's true."

Inside the yellow, warm cabin, Jay motioned to the cot.

"Sit."

He grabbed my bag and pulled out the helmet.

"Take it," he said.

I just shook my head.

"Leo, I wouldn't make you do this if it weren't incredibly important."

I reached out and took the helmet in my hands. It was the same as before. The shocking bolt of electricity, followed by the lights, the suction, the darkness and the tide, the popping sounds like frying bacon and its little fireflies. The tremendous speed as I approached the swirling purple whirlpools, the clicks, the squeaks, the little hands on clean glass, the door creaking open and shut. The immense freedom and emotions as I became one of them. And then the crushing sadness as I felt the strands between us melt into thin air, as only that one little purple whirlpool swirled in front of me. It was just a baby. Then I heard it, the cry, the scream that crashed over me in wave after wave, filling all the space, becoming me, until I was alone in the space, trembling in sadness and fear.

"That's enough, Leo!" Jay's echoey voice boomed, pulling the helmet out of my hands. "You don't have to go through that anymore. I heard it. I understand now. I understand . . . "

I slumped down into the cot and clamped my hands over my ears, trying to recover. My head was throbbing. My heart was pulsing, like waking up from a nightmare. I shut my eyes and just tried to breathe. When I finally looked up, I saw Jay across the cabin, standing by the radio equipment, his head bowed and his tan, leathery hand covering his eyes.

"What have I done? What have I done?" he kept muttering over and over again.

"What happened, Jay? Did I do something wrong?"

"No, Leo, you're innocent. I'm the guilty one. I've worked for almost thirty years to make up the wrongs that I committed doing my experiments, but now I see that I can never escape from what I have done."

"What do you mean, how could any of this be your fault?"

"Leo, the sound you heard from the helmet was a baby dolphin, a calf. It was its signature call. Every dolphin has one — we don't know what they really mean, but we think it's like their names. And every dolphin gets one by imitating its mother's call. That very humanlike call you heard was what I taught them. No other dolphin in the world made that sound. Only the seven I trained."

"But it was a baby," I said. "He was in pain; I felt it."

"Yes, he was in pain. He was crying out for his mother. In the voice that he learned from her. In the voice she learned from me."

"Was the baby the one that wore the helmet?" I asked. "Is that why he was in pain?"

"I don't know, Leo, but I don't think so. When I abandoned my experiments, I trusted a friend to find a good home for the seven dolphins I trained. Back then, there was no place like my reserve. We hadn't learned yet. My friend must have sold them to the highest bidder, while I was locked away in my isolation tank. There's always someone willing to pay for a trained dolphin. Obviously, he sold them to the military. And tricked once again by man, they had to wear those awful helmets."

Jay looked like a beaten man. "I'm just like the rest of them," he said softly.

I didn't know what to say. His grief was so deep. I wanted to jump across the cabin and hug him the way he'd hugged me, but I couldn't.

I left the cabin and stepped outside, leaving Jay alone with his thoughts.

CHAPTER 25

Jay stayed in the cabin for the rest of the trip. I joined Trevor on deck. We sat on the bow, and eventually we watched the sunrise together in silence. As the sun rose higher in the sky, Trevor jumped to his feet.

"Land ho!" he shouted. "There!"

I followed his finger across the ocean to a yellowish hazy blob no bigger than my pinkie. I squinted at it. The sky around it seemed almost brown.

I called for Jay, and we all gathered at the wheel while Cal examined the map. Jay looked through the binoculars, then handed them to me. I scanned the horizon until that yellowish mound was in my view. The glob of land was a sickly shade of yellow, with spotted rust-colored patches of barren earth. There wasn't a tree anywhere. I handed the binoculars back to Jay.

"I believe this repulsive eyesore is Makuna," Jay said, as he passed the binoculars to Becky.

"It looks like a war zone out there," she said, giving the binoculars to Trevor.

"Or one of Jupiter's moons," he added. "Io, the volcanic wasteland, my favorite Jovian satellite."

We were drawing closer to it. And the closer we got, the more the air felt hard and heavy, and the water turned from the pure blue to that greenish color of the East River. I had an awful feeling in the pit of my stomach.

"Lower the sails to half-mast," Cal barked.

Becky followed his command and as the sail dropped down the mast, the boat slowed.

I looked through the binoculars again and watched the narrow spit of land emerging. I still couldn't find any trees. Broken concrete slabs and twisted metal rods were scattered across the rocky terrain. I saw a small path leading to a few crumbling concrete buildings on the far side of the island. They were obviously long abandoned. A rusted-out jeep was lying on its side looking like a dead metal animal.

"Do you think this was an army base?" I asked Jay, still looking through the binoculars.

"Maybe. But probably a military weapons site. Back in the day, they did a lot of nuclear and chemical weapons testing on islands like this. I believe we are looking at a military experiment gone out of control. One more ghost of war."

I lowered the binoculars. We were practically on top of the island, and it rose several hundred feet into the air, towering over us. Concrete slabs with jagged metal bars, like the ones scattered over the island, jutted out from the shallow water and surrounded our drifting boat like a minefield. The air surrounding us was oppressive.

A rusty piece of barbed wire scraped along the hull and got caught on the protective wire of our boat, right next to me, and made a hideous scraping sound. I reached out to remove it, but as soon as I touched it, a bolt of current ran through me and I heard sounds. Dozens of machines churning, the faraway noise of airplane engines, several thuds from an explosion, men's voices shouting in another language.

"What, Leo?" Trevor whispered. He'd come to realize when I was sound bending.

He pulled my hand off the barbed wire, but it tore away a chunk of skin from my palm. It stung, and then blood started to fill in the missing chunk.

"Explosions," I groaned to Trevor. "Angry men, voices . . . "

"Ooh, that's a nasty cut," Becky said. "Don't suck on it, it needs disinfectant." She hurried down into the cabin to get a first-aid kit.

It stung sharply, and it didn't look good.

"Dangle it in the water, Leo," Trevor said. "The salt water is cleansing."

"Are you crazy? I've got enough pain in my life."

"Better than worrying about Crane."

I plunged my hand into the green water, resting it on one of the concrete fragments near the hull, and a jellyfish-like sting shot into my hand, then coursed through my veins. Suddenly, the concrete slabs and twisted metal wires seemed to grow and move like they were all a part of one terrible organism. What was this place? Where was I? I heard that cry echoing through everything I saw, as if one giant form of life was making this sound. But it wasn't just one cry. There were others. Everywhere I looked in this miserable world the cries echoed, each different, each moving and pulsing with an alien energy. Pulsing in this strange harsh light, in this murky water seeded with the twisted ghosts of war. "Where are you, Daddy?" I heard myself scream from far away, in a voice almost like that human wail of those dolphins.

"Daddy, where are yoooooouuuuuuuuu?"

Suddenly, another hand was on mine, yanking it out of the water as I came back into myself and away from that horror. It was Trevor. Jay was watching, observing me with a mixture of concern and scientific curiosity.

"You were sound bending?" Jay asked.

I nodded.

"And you called out for your father."

"There's so many of them," I gasped. "They're everywhere. I can't face it alone."

"Leo," Jay said, lowering his head to my eye level, and focusing his entire person on me. "There comes a time when a boy has to become his own father. Your time has come much too soon, but here it is. Trust that you have a lot of him already in you."

He reached out to pinch my cheek, but I shook my head. "I'm okay," I said, as I took a breath and looked straight at Jay.

"You said 'them,' Leo?" Trevor asked.

"There's more than one dolphin down there. I heard them and I'm going to find them."

"Leo, you don't know *what's* out there," Trevor objected. "It isn't safe here."

I looked at everything around me and shook my head. I'd seen countless war movies on TV, but war never looked like this before. Still, I knew what I had to do.

"Listen, Trev. I don't know why I have this power, but there has to be a reason. I have serious work to do in this world and I can't be a scared little kid anymore."

I saw Jay nodding his head in agreement and a proud smile crossed his lips.

"There's not enough time," Trevor argued. "Crane will be getting to the island soon. And he'll find a way to get here."

"If he finds us, he finds us. But not before I find them."

We were all quiet for a long time, then Jay said simply, "I'm going with you."

Becky equipped us with snorkels, masks, and flippers. She said she'd stay on the boat and keep a lookout. Even she was afraid of this place.

Jay went into the water first, and I slipped in after him. Almost immediately, my body was covered with a greasy film. Jay told me to stay in his sight at all times, so I made sure he was still in mine. The man was a natural in the water—he glided like one of the dolphins in the cove. But this water wasn't like the pure blue water in his lagoon. It was foul. Oily particles and flecks of gunk clung to my goggles. The sea floor, only ten feet deep here, was lined with a gray sludge. Underwater, all I heard were faint air bubbles, the swirling water from my flippers, and my own strange hollow breaths from the snorkel. No other sounds of life, just a haunting silence.

We were surrounded by those pillars of concrete, jagged and ripped apart, their metal wires jutting out in all directions. Flimsy, transparent green leaves clustered around them and quivered in the current. I looked over at Jay, and he pointed at me, indicating that he was going to follow me. This was my mission, he was telling me. I had to lead the way. The way to what? All I had to go on was that sound in my head, but where was it leading me? I was lost.

I simply let myself float on the current and opened my vision up to the ocean beneath me. I couldn't see life at all — only the gray sludge that rose up in cloudy plumes at the slightest current and those pathetic wispy sea leaves, so transparent they seemed like they would dissolve into the sludge with even the softest touch. Something had happened here, something terrible. All of the life had been sucked out of the place with such force and violence that there was no music, no sound. Just the dreadful silence. The sound of my hollow breathing through the snorkel gave me the impression that I was in a space suit on another planet. But no, this was Earth.

This must have been what the hallelujah man envisioned when he had his bad days, when he screamed down the block, "Can't you see it's all junk? It's all garbage?"

I was next to one of the concrete structures, the only one not broken into fragments. It was a solid rectangle of concrete that rose from the sludge and jutted out of the ocean to a spot three feet above the surface. Below the surface there was a square opening, big enough for me to swim into. I touched the concrete, and suddenly, every part of me was tingling with fear, my heart thumping in my throat. As I withdrew my hand, I knew this was it. Could I actually go in?

I popped to the surface and treaded water as I cleaned my mask. Jay was by my side. He had followed me the whole time.

"I'm going to go in there," I told him, pointing to the black square on the side.

"Okay, Leo. Take some deep dolphin breaths and fill your lungs with plenty of oxygen."

I did. I breathed slowly and deeply, to try to calm myself. And as I listened to my own breath, the memory of my father breathing on that blue disc came to my mind. That memory was all that I had in this waste. From his breath to mine. I dove.

I was in a concrete room. It was about ten feet down and maybe seven feet across, hard to tell because it was so dark in there. There was a little pocket of air on the surface below the concrete roof. The walls were crusted with sludge and flaky yellow globs. I had seen enough war movies to know that this was a bunker. The floor was concrete, too, covered with mounds of oily black sand. To my surprise, I saw beautiful shiny things scattered over it, sparkling glimmers rising from this murky cave. I dove down to get a better look. They were shards of coral. My air was running out, so I flipped around to swim out of the hole and to the surface.

Just as my chest felt ready to burst, I saw that my flipper had kicked up a cloud of dust, and uncovered something else on the floor.

I gasped the foul air on the surface outside and caught my breath.

"See anything?" Jay asked.

"Coral," I said, still breathing heavily. Before he had time to ask, I filled my lungs and dove back into the bunker. It was dark and cloudy in there, but I knew what that was on floor. I saw bones. Half buried in the corner. As I dove closer, I realized I was looking at the crumbling skeleton of a long creature. Ribs and spiny vertebrae still intact. And attached to them was a skull. The hollow dark cavities of its eyes stared out at me. A long beak with rows of white teeth curving back into a smile. It was a dolphin.

Suddenly, I felt that weird zap of energy ran up and down my spine, and then a red light came on, filling the bunker with an eerie submarine glow. It was just enough light for me to see the helmet sitting atop the dolphin's skull. It was identical to the one in Crane's warehouse, the one I had brought to the island. I swam close enough to make out the same rows of braided wires and the clawlike needles that were still inserted into the hollow skull where there had once been a mind. If this skeleton was my purple light friend, the brother I was supposed to save, then he was already dead. The shards of coral glimmered in the red light from the blinking helmet, and I rose to the air pocket within the bunker to catch my breath, feeling like I was going to throw up.

I knew this wasn't all there was to it. That sadness I felt that day in Crane's warehouse in Brooklyn, that sadness that led me all the way here, couldn't have been just for those bones in here. I kept thinking about the sound of my breathing, and my dad's from that recording. From an island of birth to an island of death — was that all? No, it couldn't be.

I dove back into the water, and as I went deeper, I heard something new — an insistent *beep, beep, beep*. I swam toward the helmet and the sound grew louder. It was painfully shrill in my ears — like a thousand grocery store scanners playing a high-pitched symphony. The helmet was making that sound. *Beep, beep, beep*. Inserting itself into the silence.

I can find music in every sound, but there was none in that one, only misery. How different that helmet was from the theremin that Hollis played. One made music. The other made pain. One brought people together. The other separated them forever.

Just then something smooth glided across my back, something slippery, electric. As it touched me, I saw the purple whirlpool of light flash in front of my eyes, and heard its wail in my mind's ear. I had company. I spun around and there he was — a gray dolphin, alone and powerful inside the bunker with me. But he wasn't here to see me. He swam to the bones, whistling and clicking at the red light. The machine changed tones, and beeped back to him. I rose to the surface of the bunker and floated there, my snorkel sucking in the fetid air.

Had that zap I felt been a sonar beam from the dolphin,

turning on the helmet, or somehow, had that cry inside of me turned it on? I didn't have time to think about it. More dolphins swam in through the hole, four of them of all different sizes, including a baby that swam close behind its mother. They whistled and chirped at the helmet, and when they were all inside, every one in the pod made that humanlike wail, one at a time, one after the other, just like on Jay's record. Just like I had heard in my bedroom as a small child.

Then why wasn't I afraid? That cry was still there in my mind, but it was different now, changed. I still heard that sadness, but mostly now what I heard was a deep desire to communicate. To build a bridge to their cousins on dry land. To leap across time and build a bridge to their dead ancestor. To say, I am here. To sing, we come in peace.

I heard Jay calling my name through the concrete walls. I took the sight in one last time and dove through the square in the wall.

"Leo!"

"You have to see this, Jay!"

"I watched the whole thing, Leo! I would have never believed it."

"We found them, Jay!"

"I think so, Leo!"

"But why are they still here?"

"Sometimes, when and individual is stranded, the rest of the pod won't leave the area."

Just then there was a splash fifty feet away from us. Two of the dolphins glided through the air, the drops of water casting hundreds of miniature rainbows. And then they cried out to us, cried out to us with a humanlike wail. How many times had they cried out in despair, with only this zombie life to hear them? Then another one breached by Jay and clicked and squeaked and brushed up against him. Jay put his hand on her torso and she cried out to him through her blowhole.

"Hey, old girl!" He laughed back to her. I was laughing, too.

"Is she one of your old ones?"

"If only, Leo. But she is an old one, all right."

Then he put on his mask and dove beneath the water and swam and played with her, bobbing up above the surface, the sound of splashes and laughter filling this harsh air.

Becky and Trevor and Cal were screaming from the boat, jumping up and down and laughing at us.

"Cheers, mate!" Cal yelled. "Real beaut!"

"Jay, you found them!" Becky yelled.

"Leo found them."

The rest of the pod surfaced, slapping their tails and jumping through the air as we swam back toward the boat. They seemed to be following us.

Becky, Trevor, and Cal helped us onto the boat and out of our gear. Jay and I were covered from head to toe in goop, like those pelicans on the Gulf Coast. We all just sat on the deck and watched them play.

"Do you think any of those are your research dolphins, Jay?" I asked.

"Unfortunately no, Leo. These are their children. And grandchildren! No helmets on any of them."

"What's going to happen to them?" Trevor asked.

"I'll tell you, Trevor," Becky said. "I am going to camp on this island until we can get a fully equipped rescue operation here. Then if they want to come, we can take the whole pod back to the reserve. And we're going to send cameras here, and tape recorders, and document and study what happened here."

"I'll stay with you, Becky," Trevor volunteered. "I'm an excellent camper."

She just smiled at him and gave him a tiny little kiss on the forehead. Trevor's long, skinny legs wobbled like a baby goat's.

"Someday soon, you'll make a special woman very happy."

Trevor grinned at her like an idiot, but not for long.

"Be sure to give Jeremy my e-mail address, okay?" she said to him. "Tell him I said he *might* even be worth a trip to New York for me."

Poor Trevor. You could practically hear his ego deflating.

We gathered all our provisions and packed a waterproof bag for Becky. As she dove into the water, Trevor promised to e-mail her every day when he got home.

We watched her swim toward the shore. And when she reached dry land, Cal started barking at us again, and within moments we had gotten the *Flipper* ready for the return trek.

We set sail. I stayed near the rear and watched Makuna fade into the distance, until it was just that yellow glob on the horizon and then was out of sight. I thought of my favorite kung fu movie. The hero sneaks into a Shaolin temple after his family has been murdered by a warlord.

The training is intense. He has to go through all these different training chambers — each more punishing than the last — to become a master, and it takes years. When he becomes the best kung fu master in the whole temple, he decides to start his own training chamber outside of the Shaolin temple. The monks were furious: Their kung fu was a secret; nobody outside the temple was supposed to learn it. But this guy didn't care. He chose to teach the people, so they could protect themselves against all the cruel warlords out there. That was the way he chose to use his power. And now as I sat with my feet dangling in the warm ocean, I knew that this was what I had been called to do with my own power. These dolphins may not have called out to me, but I had listened, and I always would.

By my feet there were several gray shapes in the water, gliding with our boat. One of the shapes shook himself back and forth and darted way ahead of the group and leapt into the air in front of us, spinning around in a perfect circle. A dolphin! Everyone cheered and screamed.

"Are those ours, Jay?"

"No, Leo," he yelled out, laughing. "Those are spinner dolphins." Another one spun in the air ahead of us, like he was performing a special show just for us. "Look at that one! There's nothing in the world that dolphins love more than sailboats and happy children . . . ahem . . . happy young men."

We cheered as we watched the spinners catapult themselves aloft against the sun, but soon I saw something else in flight. It was a plane, probably a private jet, and it was heading in our direction.

CHAPTER 26

We had excellent winds sailing back to Palmira, which was just the opposite of what I wanted. I needed time to make a plan, to figure out a way to tell Crane that he wasn't going to get his helmet back.

I had promised Jay he could have it. At first, he didn't want it.

"There's already one of those polluting our waters," he said. "One is more than enough."

But then the scholar in him won out, and he decided that as vile as it was, the helmet was part of dolphin history and needed to be studied, photographed, and documented.

"I have just the person to do it," he said. "Sasha Olevski."

"But he's Russian, Jay. Don't you think he'll be embarrassed by what his country did?"

"History is full of countries behaving badly," Jay said. "The important thing is for each person to do what is right. Sasha is a good man. He'll do what is right."

We clipped along in silence after that. Jay stretched out on the deck and nodded off. Trevor was busy writing notes in his notebook about everything that had happened to us. Scientific observations, he called them. I couldn't stop worrying about Crane. I knew he would be furious. That was a given. But how that anger would express itself, that was the great unknown. I had no idea what he was capable of.

The five-hour journey went by much too fast for me. When we entered the Palmira lagoon, Trevor and I got into a rowboat with Jay, while Cal dropped anchor and stayed aboard to clean the decks. Jay rowed easily, despite his age. Trevor sat with his back to the island, clutching the duffel bag with the helmet inside. And I kept scanning the land, hoping against hope that I wouldn't see Crane anywhere.

No such luck.

A peculiar shiny flare caught my eye from the shore, and with it, the entire beauty of Palmira felt threatened by a dark force. The shiny flare was coming from a shiny bald head. The shiny bald head belonged to Crane. He was wearing a black suit, probably the only person ever to wear one on the island. He was pacing back and forth in the Pod. I could see Jeremy sitting at a nearby table, holding his head in his hands like he had a terrible headache.

"Crane looks ready to explode," I whispered to Trevor.

Jay stopped rowing long enough to observe Crane. "How could a person like that be related to your father?" he said, shaking his head.

"My dad and he were stepbrothers."

"Ah, no shared DNA. That makes slightly more sense."

Jay picked up the oars again, but I begged him to row slowly, hoping for extra time to go over my explanation to Crane. Trevor told me to just be logical and firm, and explain to him why we took the helmet.

"Staying calm is the key," Trevor said. "Use your head. Don't let your emotions get in the way."

I didn't feel calm.

We docked the rowboat and got out, Trevor holding the duffel behind his back. When Jeremy saw us, his face lit up. He got up and charged down the hill. Crane yelled after him.

"Where do you think you're going, you lazy hippie?"

"Who's the little guy coming out of the kitchen?" Jay asked. I was so busy watching Crane that I hadn't noticed that there was someone else with him.

"Hollis!" I screamed. "Hey, bro, over here!"

Of course, by then, Crane had seen us. He tried to restrain Hollis from coming to meet us, but Hollis wrested himself away from Crane's grip. He sprinted down the path as Trevor and I bolted toward him. Suddenly, I wasn't even thinking about the serious trouble I was in with Crane. All I could think about was how great it was to see Hollis. I gave him a big hug.

"Crane's ranting about you being a thief," Hollis whispered. "What'd you steal?"

"Something he had no right to have."

"Dmitri said you dudes bagged something pretty valuable."

Trevor and I exchanged glances. We really didn't need proof that Dmitri was a snitch for Crane, but if we ever had, there it was.

"Uh-oh. Here he comes," Hollis said. "You're toast."

Crane marched up to me, taking long, angry strides, until his face was right next to my face. I could see him sweating.

Okay, I thought, time to see what I'm made of.

"Well, if it isn't my nephew, the little thief," he said, his voice crackling with rage. "The one who feels he can help himself to another man's possessions. The one who sneaks off with an artifact worth half a million dollars."

"It's no artifact," I said. "That helmet is an instrument of torture. Do you know what they used it for?"

"I don't care, Leo." Crane was yelling now. "I am not in the business of asking questions that don't pertain to me. The only questions I ask are 'How much will you pay?' and 'When can I have my money?'"

"You shouldn't be selling a thing like that," I yelled back. "It's wrong."

"Well, Leo, I'm afraid your little piece of juvenile advice is too late. Some Russian businessmen are waiting for it. It's already sold."

"They just want to cover up what their country did. Do you know there are needles inside that helmet?" My voice was rising in anger now. I could hear it quivering as I talked. "Do you know what those needles did? They went into the dolphins' brains. Can you even understand what that did to them? Can you?"

"Leo, you are acting like an hysterical child," Crane said. "Bad things happen in this world. One person cannot fix everything."

"That's no reason not to try. You can tell those crooks you deal with that they can't have their helmet. I'm not giving it back. Not for any amount of money."

Crane's face turned the red color of his tie. The veins in his neck stuck out so far they looked like fingers.

"This is outrageous!" he bellowed. "Do you realize what you've cost me, Leo?"

We were attracting quite a bit of attention from the workers, who had just finished lunch. A woman passing by had a tray with some glasses of lemonade on it. She held it out for Crane and the rest of us.

"Get that away from me!" he yelled, knocking the tray out of her hand. Then he turned to the rest of the volunteers and workers who had gathered around. "All you fish lovers helped him do this. You participated in this crime. You're responsible as well. I have a good mind to shut this place down. Buy all your land and put up a hotel. A high-rise with Jet Skis and motorboats. That would scare away all your precious dolphins."

"I'm afraid that's impossible," Jay said, stepping forward in his tiny blue swimsuit. He had been listening quietly until then. Now he spoke with authority, his voice strong and clear. "We own the deed to this land. And I'd like to ask you to leave the property at once, sir."

"You're Lylo, right?" Crane turned to face him. "My good man, you go about dressed like that? I was under the impression these boys were coming here to learn science."

"They were," Jeremy said.

"And they did," Jay added. "They learned how the awful helmet in that bag works. They learned about dolphin echolocation. And they learned above all that science was not invented to do harm."

Crane wasn't listening to Jay. All his attention was focused on the bag in back of Trevor. Jay had let the secret slip out. Crane knew the helmet was in there.

He took a step toward Trevor and clenched his jaw into a snarl. Little rivers of sweat were pouring down his bald head.

"Give me that bag immediately," he said, tapping Trevor hard on the chest.

"Hand it to me, Trev," Jeremy said. Trevor passed the bag to Jeremy, who looked square into Crane's eyes.

"I just think people should pick on someone their own size," he said.

"This doesn't concern you, *Ponytail*. This is family business."

"Kirk was like a father to me. That's close enough." Then, turning to me, he asked, "Leo, what do you want to do with the helmet? Legally, it doesn't belong to you. But you know what they say . . . possession is nine-tenths of the law."

"I'm not giving it back. It belongs to science now."

Jeremy shrugged and smiled at Crane.

"You heard the man," he said.

"All right, Leo. You win." Crane's eye was twitching as he spoke. "The helmet is yours."

"You bet it is," I said, tasting victory.

"You didn't hear me out, Leo. The helmet is yours, and now I'm officially offering to buy it from you for fifty thousand dollars."

"Don't do it, Leezer," Trevor whispered.

"One hundred thousand," Crane said. "And that's my final offer."

"No way," Trevor said.

"Are you his business manager?" Crane asked.

"I'm his friend."

"How touching."

Crane sighed deeply. I could see his calculator of a brain shift into gear.

"Fine. I only do this is in memory of my beloved brother. I will deposit two hundred and fifty thousand dollars into an account with your name on it, Leo, when you turn over that helmet to me."

"Two hundred and fifty thousand dollars," Hollis repeated. "That's enough for a down payment on a yacht."

"In addition, I'll pay your gangly friend here twenty-five thousand dollars, for his role as your . . . ahem . . . business manager. It's a fair deal. A win-win for everyone involved."

"Except for me," Hollis said. "What do I get?"

I shot Hollis a disapproving glance, but Crane actually looked pleased.

"I like your style, Hollis. I'll put the two hundred and fifty thousand in both your names, if that meets with the approval of your brother. What do you say, Leo? Show me you're as smart as I hope you are."

Everyone was silent as I tried to do math with numbers too big to understand.

"What are you waiting for?" Crane asked. "You'd be a fool to say no."

"Leo, we have to talk about this," Hollis whispered to me. "We're in this together. Half that money is mine."

"We leave in one hour," Crane said. "You, Hollis, your gangly friend, myself, and the helmet. I'll be waiting at that pathetic excuse for a restaurant."

As Crane marched back to the shade of the Pod, he turned to the woman in the flowered skirt. "I'll have that lemonade now. Two sugars, lots of ice."

"Why don't you boys talk?" Jay said. "I'll come find you in half an hour."

I took Hollis and Trevor and we climbed the path up to the cliff overlooking the cove. When we arrived, we sat down in a circle, like a Native American tribal council. Trevor placed the helmet in the middle of our circle. The ocean breeze blew strong and salty, and the view down to the beach was perfect.

It was an impossible decision. I felt it was wrong to make money off of that helmet and profit from the evil that it had done. Besides, I had promised it to Jay. On the other hand, it had served its purpose. We had found the dolphins. I had found my powers.

Two hundred and fifty thousand dollars was a lot of money. A cool quarter of a million. Hollis pointed out that it would pay for him to make a record, and try to become the rock star he always dreamed of being. It would help pay for college for both of us, so we wouldn't have to rely on Crane. I could study sound or dolphins or anything I wanted. Trevor's share would help his mom not have to work all night, every night.

I went back and forth, trying to sort out what I felt was right. In the end, Trevor said it was up to me, and even Hollis agreed. The minutes were ticking away, and we would be leaving the island soon. The question was . . . would I be leaving with the helmet or without it?

As the hour drew close, I still didn't know the answer.

CHAPTER 27

ay climbed up the hill to where we sat.

"It's time, men. You'd better hurry."

He reached into his dive bag and pulled out three large, spiral seashells and handed one to each of us. They were rough and pink on the outside, pearly and smooth on the inside.

"A little something to remember us by," he said. "When you hold these shells to your ear, you'll hear the roar of the ocean. We'll all be there with you. Tami and Freddy, too. Look, they came to say good-bye."

When I looked down into the cove, I could see the pod of dolphins, splashing and playing. Tami and Freddy were showing off, bobbing up and down in the water like buoys.

Man, were they ever cute and innocent. I imagined

the dolphins of Makuna Island, our dolphins, playing in the lagoon one day, restored to health by Jay and his fellow scientists.

That image made me smile, filled me with happiness, in fact.

I ran back and picked up the helmet. Closing my eyes, I held it tight against my body. A bolt of lightning shot through me, and then the sounds started to bend in my secret ears. I heard my whole adventure unravel before me, only this time, I understood it. The darting swirls of light. The human-like voices, calling for help, for love and comfort. Along with that sound came a tremendous feeling of longing — the longing to reach out and touch a parent who was no longer there. I knew that feeling. I knew it for me and I knew it for the dolphins who still, so many years later, were carrying bits of coral to their mother's grave. Preserving her memory in their wonderful minds.

I opened my eyes, and though my head was pounding and my legs were weak, I walked over to the ledge. I knew what I had to do. Everything felt right about it. There was no decision, only the loud, clear call of my heart speaking to me.

I ran toward the edge of the cliff and heaved the helmet as hard as I could. It wobbled in the air, then dropped down and smashed into the rocky ledge below, splintering into pieces. Shards of plastic and metal flew here and there, until the helmet was no longer recognizable. It would never harm a living being again.

I felt free.

Crane was waiting at the jeep as we made our way down the hill. He strode up to me with a confident look and held out his hand for the duffel bag.

"I'm glad to know that reason has prevailed, Leo. Hand me the bag and we'll be on our way."

I handed him the bag. He could tell immediately that it was empty.

"Where is it, Leo? Where is my helmet?"

"In about a thousand pieces."

"First you steal my property and then you destroy it!"

Crane wheeled around and grabbed Hollis by the arm.

"I thought I could count on you to talk some sense into your empty-headed brother. That's why I brought you. Dmitri said you were someone to be trusted."

"Leo did what he believed was right," Hollis said. "You got to respect that."

"Maybe you got to, but I don't got to." Crane was livid. He spun around to face Jay, and I was afraid he was actually going to punch him out. His hands were balled up into fists as he spoke.

"You put him up to this," he said. "You and your high morals. Well, look where those morals have gotten you. Stuck on this excuse for an island with your loser squad and your smelly fish. I pity you."

"And I you," Jay said.

Crane stomped off and got into the jeep. Sweat was dripping down the sides of his face.

"Are you going to be okay?" Jay asked, turning to me.

"I'm going to give it my best shot. How can I ever thank you, Jay?" I held out my hand to him, but he pushed it aside and gave me a big hug instead.

"You're a fine man, Leo. You can do a lot of good in this world of ours."

His blue eyes were filled with tears as we said good-bye.

We all climbed into the jeep, Trevor, Hollis, Jeremy, and I, all squeezing into the backseat because no one wanted to be up front with Crane. We could hear him breathing like an animal all the way along the shoreline road to the plane.

It wasn't easy sitting on that plane for twenty hours, with Crane not speaking to anyone, just sitting there silently, except for the sound of his pinkie ring clicking against the tray table. Once, somewhere over Hawaii, he looked at me and said, in a tone of voice that was colder than icicles, "You're just like your father, Leo."

"Thank you," I said.

Hollis stifled a laugh, and Crane shot him a filthy look.

"I have higher hopes for you, Hollis. I hope you'll grow up to appreciate the value of money."

I had higher hopes for Hollis, too. I hoped he'd grow up to be just who he was meant to be. He had a little voice in his head, a musical one, and I knew if he paid attention to it, he was bound to make some great music. I couldn't wait to get home and tell him what I had learned about Dad. I had gone all this way, but he was half of the record I'd been looking for. I was the other half. Our shared memories of our parents were the music.

I must have fallen asleep because somewhere over the Rocky Mountains, I startled awake from what I thought was turbulence. But it wasn't turbulence that woke me. It was Crane, staring at me with his angry eyes. I could feel them even in my sleep.

"You know I have half a mind to send you away for what you've done," he said. "There are boarding schools, you know. Places where insolent young men like you are sent when they can't get along at home."

It was the first thing he ever said that truly terrified me. I couldn't bear the thought of being separated from Hollis. He was all I had left of my family.

"Please, don't do that," I said softly. "My father was counting on you to look after us. You promised him."

"I don't care about those silly promises," Crane said. "However, I do care about the lost mask of Long Pulung. I care about that very much."

It seemed like forever ago that Crane had first opened the muddy burlap bag to show me the soul-catcher mask he had found among my dad's things.

"My research is promising," he said. "You might be useful in my search for the twin mask."

I knew in my heart that I would never want to help Crane, but it was handy to make him think I would. At least, it meant that I could stay with him, stay with Hollis, stay in New York where my memories were.

"So I don't have to go away?"

"Not yet. But I wouldn't get too comfortable if I were you."

Crane sat back down in his chair, put on his sleeping mask, and gave me the silent treatment the rest of the way.

Stump was waiting for us on the private jetway. As we climbed into the back of the limo, he pulled me aside.

"How'd it go, kiddo?"

"Okay," I said. "I was afraid but I did what I had to do."

"You showed 'em," he said, and reached into his pocket and handed me a new red straw. "Keep this handy."

We dropped Trevor off at his building, then headed over the bridge to Brooklyn. The sky was light orange and purple. It was either twilight or dawn, I couldn't tell. I had no idea what time it was, or even what day. Hollis was asleep, his head resting on my shoulder. I leaned back and listened to the sounds of the city — the taxi horns, the street cleaner, the wind whipping through the cables of the Brooklyn Bridge.

So much had happened to me. Was it only a week ago that I had turned thirteen and found the blue disc? Nothing in my life was the same. Except for the rhythmic *bump, ba bump, bump ba bump* of the tires rolling over the bridge. I turned my head toward the magical light swirling off the East River and the deep ocean beyond, and I smiled. I knew that this was where I was supposed to be. That right here was home. The world is a place made out of music, and I would use my power to help people remember those bridges that connect us all.

The melody of my ancestral name played in my secret ears, and I heard every note of it in full stereo sound. It was my song. It was our song. It was the melody of the universe.

I am Leo Lomax, the bridge between worlds. I am Sound Bender.